CODE JUNKIE
By Jeffrey Koval Jr.

To friends and family, past, present, and future.

INTRODUCTION

You never know when the end of your tale will suddenly find you.

Sometimes it's the drink; sometimes, the cancer. Perhaps you live a charmed existence, follow three squares a day and get plenty of exercise, much like our world's beloved inmates, and find yourself on the underside of an eighteen-wheeler crossing a busy street that you could have sworn was vacant just moments earlier. We will openly live in fear of the latest pandemic that is sweeping the streets, yet refuse to wash our hands upon exiting a public restroom. We will continue eating in restaurants, shaking hands with strangers, kissing babies. Yet were you to act upon such primitive self-contingency impulses to act differently, you would be branded the hermit, the mentally-insane, the broken, the man who washes his hands too much and carries around disinfectant sprays.

We all absolutely love to dwell on nonsense and write our own afterlives, forge our own outline of the universe, and create a unique perspective, just like every other poor bastard before us. The religious worship their deities and their pieces of wood or porcelain and the atheists stake their claim that our bodies simply turn off the lights. But we all end up in a wooden box, in pieces on a busy street, lost at sea, or some beautiful combination of the three that makes for one hell of an obituary. I am pretty sure I am not going to fulfill such a colorful destiny (pity, I know) but not even my bloodline has escaped the curse of willing oneself to believe that they know what happens upon death and what causes our beating bodies to experience it. My grandmother told me that we die when we lose the ability to love. Had I been ten years older upon hearing this whimsy, I would have piped in with, "Yes, Grandma, heart failure is bad," but, alas, I am simply left with a memory that leaves a dull, crooked smile and an unshakeable sensation of what a happier person would label as l'esprit del l'escalier.

1

I would be haunted with the unrelenting ability to act as a scholar in the field of human mortality. No, I hadn't any interest in the subject of biology or funeral preparations, but, as every sapping soul that has felt your skin knows well, from your mother to the coroner, you never know what ability, or gift, or talent you may be dealt upon entering this great blue world of ours.

I am standing in line at a convenience store as we speak. My dull companion Jerry is making small talk with the cashier. Jerry's curls (such an unfortunate pairing of words…) and Pillsbury demeanor cracked years off of his identity, and, living a lifestyle that more adequately held a labeling of "man-child" (rather than boy or man), led to him inadvertently becoming (however fantastical) emotionally interested in young women who were not necessarily, how shall we say, legal.

They were both smiling into each other's awkwardly spaced teeth. Jerry was saying something about the fictitious history of the popular science fiction icon on her tight, faded t-shirt, and she laughed, appreciating the reference. She was blonde, thin, and probably about seventeen years old. I looked at the register, confirmed that Jerry and I were done purchasing our wares, and slowly turned towards the large windows that fronted the store. My other travelling companion, my other co-worker, sat in his small car, still idling and shining light in the dark. Ted animatedly looked from Jerry to me and shook his head, grinning. I moved towards Jerry and touched his shoulder.

"Jer, your wife's going to be expecting us," I slurped the sugary beverage from my cup and walked towards the door. No, Jerry wasn't married, he didn't even have a girlfriend, but the anxiety that I have just managed to synthetically induce would lead to the mildly obese, bumbling fool to hastily sweep his belongings off the checkout counter and follow my retreat, so we could finally leave the damn place.

It was cool outside. The autumn was coming. I quietly entered Ted's car and adjusted my coat upon sitting in the passenger seat.

"Another high school girl?" he asked.

"Yes," this made Ted laugh. "I don't think he even realizes, half the time."

"Man… when will he get it… the braces are a dead giveaway."

Ted was right. He wasn't nearly as incompetent as the other people we were forced to associate with. Maybe this is why I could bear spending time with him, and, in turn, Jerry, who was tripping out of the front door of the convenience store and rapidly making his way to the second-row doors. In a less-than-graceful display of human aptitude, he heavily placed himself into his seat and strapped his seatbelt on, although Ted was in no hurry to drive away. After Jerry breathed audibly for a few breaths and got his bearings, he mumbled, "You know, Kevin, you're an ass…"

Jerry was not a monster. He, for whatever reason, became horrendously awkward with women our age. Growing up sheltered, perhaps he felt more comfortable with younger people. Ignorance and innocence, courting one another in a race to the bottom.

"We are what we are, Jerry."

CHAPTER ONE

My name is Kevin. I graduated six years ago from the state university with a degree in computer science. Growing up, I found less and less interest in the social sciences and humanities and believed that the world had enough sociologists and artists already. Just look in your local bookstore. I found solace in the world of technology. A solid piece of hardware cannot let you down, cannot show you up for a dinner date Friday night at eight. A flawless set of code can't reject your emotional advances, can't tell you that you're "out of their league" – no, it only complies. It's so much simpler this way. A girl named Mariah was my academia-based muse.

She was my high school sweetheart and my heartbreak. She encouraged me to study during our adolescence. She is, more or less, the reason for my career. There are many things that I never could have expected to happen since those blissful years: I would be living in a 55-and-older community due to my grandmother's passing and its attached inheritance; I never started working on a video game, even though that was my first goal upon learning programming; eventually waking from a comatose state without recalling the last two months of my life. All things that I never could have anticipated.

This last year has not necessarily been conducive to honing a pleasant morale. Hell, much of my life would not have been considered a fertile ground for social growth. I was an only child. Don't get me wrong, my parents were far from terrible people—my main criticism is that they were far from any type of person. They were anonymous, just components in the family unit. I found a tinge of positive reinforcement from achieving decent grades in public school. My dear grandmother kept me on my academic edge, further bolstered by Mariah in the later years, always proudly speaking of "opportunity." Otherwise, I never had many friends, just the few who skulked around. Even today, the only people I speak to on a near-daily basis are my coworkers, from a job I no longer keep. Friends were far and few between, but kept me adequately from lunacy.

From my small home office, wedged between a kitchen and living room, various pieces of college-requisite literature, forgotten notebooks, and fragments of reclusive male teenager paraphernalia dotted the ultra-modern unit of furniture. I believe I bought the damn thing, the shelf, my freshman year of college. Long-exhausted textbooks that boasted expansive knowledge of hardware and programming languages had accrued the most dust on the shelves. I had bested those creatures the very semesters I needed them, years ago. I dreamt in script, in binary, in any language useless to human emotion.

I was good at being a computer, at wooing the inanimate.
Good enough to find a solid job shortly after graduation. I had benefits that would make a federal agent envious, I worked the standard hours and had plenty of time to screw around with coworkers. I didn't exactly abuse that last privilege. The company was a monolith of human achievement and technology. You'd recognize the name, but it does me no good to relay it now.

There, at any given hour, you could have some schmuck in a white shirt and tie rolling across the break-room and into the hallway on an exercise-ball and promptly careening into the opposite wall in an explosion of poorly handled coffee. A few fellow employees would peek their heads into the hallway from their own offices and either giggle or come out to assist the fallen warrior to his feet.

Ted, the guy in the tie who spilled his coffee in such a majestic manner, he would struggle to his feet, his previously crisp white shirt drenched with the brown liquid, and then begin a round of laughter with his fellow coworkers. "Oh, Ted!" the female employees would giggle. Our supervisor would laugh, clapping him on the back as he walked back to his workspace. And I would sit on the opposite end of the break-room, having just watched this spectacle, and think to myself that this is the secret to technological innovations: an under-populated workplace littered with adult-sized toys that would inevitably injure their physically-awkward and out-of-shape employees. These were the men and women of ability who could shape the world with their minds and tools... only after blustering through adolescence and young adulthood hindered by unyielding social and physical ineptness. I hated Ted. But he was an alright guy and was probably my best friend, by default. That was my life.

A year or two passed.

Jerry became our friend, too. Jerry suffered from your routine blend of American obesity and curly hair. He was a few years younger than Ted and I, but quickly fell into our "clique," if you will. I thought I could live and eventually die with this company. It was comfortable to no longer have to worry about the thought of pursuing a career. I would show up, numb my consciousness with a few hours of programming, watch Ted injure himself on our coffee break, and repeat. Eventually, Jerry would relieve Ted of these masochistic comedy performances and the sound of the momentum-induced latex injuries would hit that much harder, make that much more of a noise, due to the added weight. My supervisors would always tell me to relax a bit, to enjoy myself, to feel a part of the family. I already had (and was ignored by) one of those; I felt no need to adopt yet another. Perhaps I should have bit the bullet and pretended to have listened.

I ran this comfortable routine for a few more quiet months. Jerry, Ted, and I, we each rose a bit in salary and title, but still performed the same essential tasks and still worked under the same non-essential people. The company flourished and life was sustained. Until that social-inebriant with that damned, independently-produced video game came along. Who the hell writes a blockbuster title in Java?

That blundering, overweight Swede probably thought he was the second-coming, or better. All he had to do was waltz into our office and ask politely to speak with someone from administration. He was, apparently, in town for some convention, marketing his game and swimming through throngs of his teenaged fans. Well, our human resources loved him, too. They drooled, they kissed the ground he walked on (in crummy black European sneakers), they offered him beverages, drinks that we absolutely did not typically have in stock at the facility.

"Feel a part of the family, Kevin," my bosses insisted.
"Relax, take it easy," they pleaded.
Jerry rolled, Ted laughed, and I died a little on the inside.

No, I simply wanted to work and return home, to continue my own work in the same vein.
But no, this damn Swede, he assumed the role, he felt a part of the family, he knew how to relax and take it easy.
I was replaced by an internet celebrity.

I wanted to murder the human resources employee who accompanied my boss at my termination meeting. My boss thanked me extensively and read through a list of projects that I had either greatly assisted on or created myself. It wasn't enough, apparently. They needed someone who would "bring up the mood" and not "frighten the female employees." Apparently, not responding to their bouts of small-talk was not conducive to a positive work environment. Damn that spiteful ounce of genetic malice that bestowed such a modernly attractive face on the soul of one who just wished to be left alone.

On my way out, a small box of my belongings tucked into the stereotypical cardboard box under arm, I ran into the Swedish programmer. He extended a hand.
"No hard feelings, eh? I saw some of your work. I'm sure you'll be fine out there--"
I punched the doughboy, my fist extending through his jaw in a beautiful sweeping motion. Security assisted me to my car. I obliged without further incident. My pale knuckles bled with the day's victory. He had a silly accent.
This was about a year ago, just barely.

I was unemployed for the first time in my life since middle school, having had numerous useless jobs throughout my schooling. I went into a mild depression. Case doctors would label this my initial "breaking point." They've considered me "troubled" for years; they've just always lacked a physical manifestation to rely on for proof. I went into a deep, deep binge. Booze, prescription painkillers stolen from my geriatric neighbors' mailboxes, laundry detergents, household cleaning chemicals, the blue stuff in the garage, anything I could get my hands on. I was the ICU's baby for a few days that month. Even through the nostalgic haze of a poor choice, I recall that one of the nurses was particularly attractive; the other, male. I remember my first day home, once I was allowed to leave the hospital.
I was still wearing my sickly white plastic wristlet, the one the hospital branded me with, and arrived home to find a bouquet of flowers, accompanied by a nervous Ted and a snacking Jerry, on my front porch. I stopped at the bottom of the two concrete stairs that served as the portal to my porch and stared at my two former coworkers. A moment passed. Then two, then three. I stood there, staring, at one and then the other, waiting for one of them to say something.
"Hi, Kevin," Ted began, shaking just a bit.
"Hello, Ted,"
Jerry took another handful of chips from the multicolored fist-sized bag he was eating from.

"Sara got these for you," Ted said and hefted the roses.
"But she had to go into work. How are you feeling?"
Ah, Sara. I could imagine her disinterested stare
intimidating high school boys who had no business in a 24-
hour convenience store at three in the morning. I remember
complimenting the curvature of her body, accented by the
store's dark blue vest, complete with nametag, years ago.
She laughed and punched me in the arm.
"Fine," I was feeling fine. I moved passed Ted, took the
flowers from his hand, and went inside. They followed me.

We then sat in my small kitchen, not speaking, for
about fifteen minutes. The flowers lay strewn across the
countertop, still in their clear plastic sheath, a small
envelope tucked in between the fistful of roses. An
obligatory "get well soon" note, invariably. Jerry was now,
too, a nervous wreck, for he had depleted his stash of
deep-fried stimulant.
"Have you… have you talked to anyone at work?" he
asked, trying to make conversation.
"Not really. They wouldn't want me back anyway. I've been
busy with other things." Such as being in the hospital, for
instance. And overdosing. That too.
"Well," he continued. "Ted and I have been looking around
for you, since before… this," Oh, great. "And apparently,
one of the engineers knew a guy who needed some help.
He's a manager for some camera company." Again,
another name you'd recognize, but it serves little purpose to
relay it here.
"I don't know a thing about cameras," I said.
"No, no," Ted came in. "It's fine. I talked to him about it,
they'd train you, you'd be good to go. This is a great
opportunity, you don't know how long it's gonna take you to
find a new job, otherwise. It's just something to get you out
of the house for now."
It was sunny outside. A bird chirped somewhere in the
woods surrounding my house.
"Fine."
They left a few hours later.

Ted left this friend's name on a piece of paper in the kitchen. A few days after my homecoming, I gave him a call. Later that afternoon, I was meeting him at the warehouse where I would work. This company was a branch of another, much larger technology company. This particular sub-division manufactured a convenient, pocket-sized, high-definition video camera. The things were handy as hell. On top of it all, they were cheap, both to make and to repair. And that's what they were going to have me be doing. For the next two weeks, I arrived at this warehouse at noon, on weekdays, and was instructed by an older man named Walter Hale, on the basic reassembling of these portable cameras. After the first hour of watching this nearly-senior citizen piece together the components, the whole thing was a breeze.

My productivity was at a premium. The hours were fine and I didn't have to play on a jungle-gym during my lunch break to fit in. It was just Walt and I, sitting in a small workshop tucked in the back of a warehouse, repairing customer returned cameras for eight hours at a time. The small talk was microscopic and the workload, tedious. It was everything I had ever wanted.

Some supervisor, whom I had only met to sign the official working papers, congratulated Walt and I on our over-the-top output a week or so in. In my mind, this was the final test of Walt's character: after the supervisor shook our hands and walked away, Walt shook his head and muttered, "Prick." I loved my job. To celebrate, we shared two deep glasses of whiskey that Walt had produced from his large bag that he kept at his feet, under his desk. I'm sure it was against some policy, written and forgotten somewhere in the company's by-laws and HR policies, but it wasn't as if we had any other visitors to worry about.

I had found financial stability once more. Walt, I never asked about his family, or any kids, or any stories from when he was in the war, or any of that useless bullshit that co-workers procure from you in the minutiae that is on-the-clock conversation. And he never bothered me with what school I went to, what I liked, if I was seeing anybody, what my family was like. None of that. It was beautiful. Although he was probably about twice my age and enjoyed a fraction of my IQ, he was my best friend.

Walt died a few weeks later.

One Monday, he didn't show up at noon. He had always been there before me, so this struck me as odd. However, I went about my business and finished my shift alone. The next two days, Walt still hadn't shown up. On Thursday, there was a card that shouted "condolences" in the breakroom, signed by our supervisor and some chance-janitor that happened to run into Walt sometime in the past year. Our boss had clipped his obituary from that morning's paper and had placed an artificial flower next to the pitiful memorial. I broke down, hysterical.

I must have terrified my supervisor. He came into the break room, saw me grieving, and moved to console me. Me, the man he never saw smile or frown, the man who shared Walt's distaste for conversation and amicability, was now hysterically sobbing at his workplace. The moment he touched my shoulder, I let out a surprised yell that sounded incredibly angry. My tears stopped. I looked him in the eye, wiped off my face, and nodded. I walked past him and back into the workroom. I sat at my desk and began to disassemble a camera that had been returned from Little Rock, Arkansas. He stood in the threshold of the break room door and stared at me, glancing back at the memorial. He wasn't going to successfully help me, so he returned to his office, his ivory tower if you will, rooms, floors even, away.

I maintained my disinterested and detached demeanor for the remainder of my shift. When I got home, I became heavily inebriated (but not enough to warrant a hospital visit) and cried myself to sleep, mourning Walt's passing.

Work was still stable, but felt different. I woke up every morning, the little multi-colored sticky notes flooding my house bearing no tangible meaning, giving no concrete direction, offering no solace. I realized that I hadn't worked on anything from home for quite some time. My computer had gathered far too many of these damn pink and yellow pieces of adhesive-lined paper. I brushed them off in the dozens from the rim of the monitor, from the edge of the keyboard, from the top of my desk. I rapidly began opening programs to quell my OCD. Homepage to my news ticker, homepage to my porn community, homepage to my video subscription feeds: check. I opened up an old project and began reviewing the code. Almost immediately, my phone rings. It was Sara.

"Hey, boozer," she monotonously panned, hinting at a giggle towards the end.

"Hey," I said.

"How's it been?"

"You know. Trying to get back into a rhythm."

"Work hasn't called you back about anything?"

"Nah. I'm gone for good. But the guys hooked me up with some camera repair job."

"Oh. That's... exciting."

"Not really."

"I know, Kevin. Regardless, we have to get together soon. I swear, I have to keep you on a goddamned leash."

"Leather?"

"Pervert."

"Alright, well, I just sat down to get some of my own stuff started—"

"Don't let me keep you, doctor. Just don't drink the alcohol in the bathroom cabinet. You'll go blind."

"Bye, Sara." She really was sometimes sweet, in her own kind of way.

I lower the phone to the desktop and move my hands to the keyboard. Yet again, almost immediately, the phone rings.

It's my boss. He needs to speak with me.
"I'll be in soon," I blankly promise.

This isn't good. It's different.

The workstations are cleared out. All of our daily supplies (pens, pieces of scrap paper, tools, etc.) are gone. My supervisor's leaning on our old table when I arrive.
"Kevin…" he begins.
       He tells me that I have nothing to really worry about, that this looks a whole lot worse than it actually is. You see, since Walt's gone, the company had finally decided that there wasn't enough man-power being hosted in our work-area to partition any more of the companies' resources towards utilities any longer. They had worked with one man back there long enough.
I offered to work in the dark. He laughed. I offered to not use the restroom. He shook his head and clapped my shoulder.
"No, Kevin, listen," he assured me. Or maybe it was more for himself. "You don't have to worry about that. We're going to have you work from home now, if you're willing," I slowly nodded. I was genuinely relieved. Images of the portly Swedish programmer flashed through my mind, haunting me. Gripping me with anger. But these quickly subsided.
"Yeah, corporate's going cut-wild, trimming where needed, you know the deal," he went on. "But we know how productive you are and we still need the customer service / repair line functioning somewhere so here we are." As if reminding himself, he fumbled in his pocket and produced a small key attached to ring.
"Since we're no longer going to be running a courier to and from our P.O. box, we'd figured that you would simply pick up the materials as a part of your duties from home."
"Sure," I agreed. He told me to come with him to his office. He'd give me the "whole picture" and I followed.

As we walked through the labyrinth of the warehouse / office complex, I noticed a great deal of aggravated-looking low-end workers giving me dirty looks. Had I become their Swedish programmer? Many of the maintenance and utilities workers were toting those iconic cardboard boxes through the halls. Some just held their boots and other tools freely. I guess the company had seriously cleaned up some of its spending. Was a shame.

We went up a few floors and arrived at my supervisor's office. I wasn't sure how high up he actually was in the company, but his office was, surprisingly, pretty nice. He had decently polished wood furniture and the like. Some reproduced painting print on the wall. The typical framed photographs on the desk, some girl around my age, presumably a girlfriend or wife.

He gave me the address of which post office they used, brief directions, (written on yet another sticky note) and the times he recommended me to pick them up. He told me that the returns and broken cameras could come in any day and in any quantity, but that it would probably be best to set up a Monday / Wednesday / Friday pick-up routine to adequately maintain a workload. I understood the logic.

He also gave me a program to install at home, that would enable me to process whose camera belonged to who and any other bureaucratic minutiae that went into keeping the accounts in check. This all was surprisingly positive.

Picking up the shipments was no big deal and the postal service took the finished orders from my house for me. It was a pretty sweet deal. I no longer had to speak to my supervisor, either, sans the occasional "How are things going?" over the phone.

I found a comfortable routine in visiting the post office. In the aisle that housed my company's shipping address, there would always be this senile old woman, regardless of the day. The post office offered three different sizes for rented-use: letter sized, medium, and large P.O. boxes. I would stroll in, unlock the large drawer that was on floor-level, place any of the post-marked cardboard boxes into a large canvas bag I brought, lock up and be on my way. This old woman, always in a bright blue sweater, would simply be staring into the gaping maw of an unlocked letter-sized P.O. box that lay ajar. Sometimes, she'd hear me approaching, turn, and give me a brief smile. Otherwise, she simply stared into the abyss.

Some days I called her Mary. Others, Gerda. Sometimes, Sally. But she never spoke. Occasionally, I would have a particularly large shipment of returns to stuff into my bag, so I would begin a one-sided conversation with the old biddy. Excellent listener, lackluster linguist. But that wasn't very surprising. I once asked her if she had seen any good movies recently. Or if she was into reading. I told her about a story I heard when I was in college, while aching through the liberal arts courses that constituted the school's core curriculum.
"Mary, did you ever hear of James Joyce's Ulysses? Read it?"

Her docile frame rocked gently to an unheard meter and her pale eyes listed towards me. Her mouth twitched a bit, open, and her non-existent response produced a small bit of drool at the corner of her bottom lip. Her eyes bore this mock-expression that I perceived as an all-around "smile" – she was an odd, empty old lady.
"Uh, Mary," I motioned towards my mouth with my hands in an animated fashion. "You have, uh, spittle," but then I waved the social cue away, realizing that she didn't know or care that she was drooling.

"Well, anyway. I haven't, either. Nah, I looked up the synopsis online and read through some criticism. Joyce seemed like a cool son of a bitch, but I just couldn't stomach that writing." Mary gently nodded and inhaled a bit of the drool.

"But, what I really loved about the guy, were the love letters he wrote to his wife. I'm serious. You listen to the radio these days, you hear nothing but terrible, mass produced rap odysseys, concerned with 'bitches' and 'ass' and whatever else these 'artists' want to spew." I rose and stood looking down towards this woman. "But James, James was dirty… but, so very… eloquent? in his lustful writing. See, I think if we taught that to our kids growing up, next to Romeo and Juliet, you know, give them both sides of the 'romantic' spectrum… I think then they'd be much more interested in reading and would actually know how to speak."

Sally still wore this almost-smile and nodded, barely picking up that I had finished talking, as if nodding was her instilled means of signifying that she was still breathing. I only then felt a bit awkward.

"It was nice talking with you, Mary." I loaded the last of the shipments and bailed.

This new job invigorated me, made me cheerful in public, made me (apparently) talkative with the mute elderly. Did this mean I would fit in at my old place now? Absolutely not. I shuddered at the thought. I wasn't at that level and I refused to ever be.

When I had arrived home, I dropped my canvas bag in my little office area and stretched both my arms out and away from my body. Arching my back, I craned my neck backwards and looked up directly through my ceiling fan, feeling the gentle breeze of its circulation. I looked back down and stepped over my bag, towards my shelf. Through the thin layers of dust, fingerprints, and a powdery blue residue, action figures and mini-statues stared back at me. I saw a particular shelf that was mostly populated by those books that had kept me company throughout my schooling years.

Fittingly enough, I found my old hardcover copy of Ulysses propped up by a small ornate Roman (or Greek) statue of a soldier, towards the end of the shelf. I picked up the little mock-bronze trinket and looked it over. Its features were pretty well-detailed for such a cheap figurine. I chucked it and traded it for the book. I stood there for a moment, staring at the cover and then opened to the first page. I began reading. Four sentences in, I made a sound that could only be described as a "pft" and replaced the damn thing on the shelf. "Not today, James."

I moved towards my desk and reached back across the room to drag my bag to my feet. With another stretch, and a content sigh, I readied myself to begin processing these latest pieces of work. Reeling back in from this second bout of stretching, I looked outside into my backyard. About twenty feet behind my property line, in the woods, I saw a small group of people walking along the small trail that led through miles of forest and eventually, a park. They were probably the area conservation group. I guess nobody really works anymore, eh. I couldn't really blame them, though. It was a beautifully mild day and their matching jackets confirmed my organizational-hypothesis. No bother.

The shelving unit kept reaching for my attention that night when I had Ted and Jerry over. A yearbook, in particular, was whispering my name and insults involving my mother.

"Now watch me as I fade into obscurity."

.

That was the epitaph I left my beloved university when they asked me for a donation upon graduation. My peers, they wrote optimistic and cheeky bits of thought that would outlive them on little (exuberantly priced) stone-bricks that were to be arranged in a memorial garden. I wondered how many of them were stricken with crippling debt and simply laughed and went along with this tired tradition that fed that all-too-human desire to immortalize yourself. I never faced such financial trials, as my immaculate public high school career inflated my worth in the eyes of prospective admission offices. I assume they were disappointed as I essentially coasted through the academic credits, never taking an outward interest in the offering of extracurricular activities or programs. The clubs always seemed boring. I do not like volunteering or tennis. Our established government in mainstream society has yet to amaze me, why in the bloody hell would I want to take part in a student-ran government. A Congress dressed in pajama bottoms with an affinity for MTV: productivity at its finest. I minded my computer science and confided in the texts. Of course, I had a few friends here and there. But one of them died in an accident and the others were in other majors, so I lost contact with them after a few years.

However, the yearbook that was stealing my concentration was from high school. It was placed right next to my college one and I needed to fact-check my personal history. For some reason, I thought of the quote on the way out the door that morning and remembered that Sara wrote it herself, signing it as an original. I wanted to see if Sara had actually written that "obscurity quote" in the margins of my yearbook or if I had simply imagined that over the years. Regardless, I felt like she was the inspiration for the message when I had, a few years after high school, left the university. I occasionally find myself wondering if anyone from those institutions remembers me fondly, if at all.

Growing up, before high school, before all of that, my grandmother was the closest thing to a best friend I had. Like I said, my parents were not awful. I suppose they just weren't exceptionally gifted at parenting, what with my father's business travel and my mother's affair with the drink. We had lived in the suburbs, well, my parents owned an empty, scarcely furnished house in the suburbs, but I spent most of my days at my grandmother's rancher home about forty minutes away (read: went to visit, rarely returned home for the week).

I wasn't even a consideration when my grandfather had passed away, but I felt as if I knew the man. He fought in multiple wars, saw parts of the world that I had yet to even learn about. Their house was of modest proportions and nestled towards the back of a long, sloping development. Much of the furnishing was further ornamented by the relics of a relatively successful marriage. Portraits, army medals, vacation photographs, and other useless pieces of garbage dotted the quaint single-story house. Situated at the back of the development, their house rested on a dense tree line. You could walk for about a half an hour into the woods and then find the forest opening up into a vast stretch of land, untouched for years.

Walking in the other direction, you could just get lost in the forest. When I had first discovered the expanse, I assumed it to be derelict farmland, driven to obsolescence by industry.

Of course, this realistic approach simply wouldn't do for the fabled charm of my grandmother. These barren lands quickly evolved into a retelling of my grandfather's tour in North Africa during the war. I guess the dirt and dust jogged her memory. Looking back through adult eyes, it's easy to see where my families' factual history and my grandma's whimsical revisions broke apart from one another.

Tales of grandpa meandering through local bazaars, making the veiled women blush and the men grow tired of his antics, of him finding precious antiques and handmade jewelry that sparkled in the African sun… all found some root in legitimacy, but the tales of him outthinking native wizards and snake-charmers, I was not so sure of. One piece I remember from the old rancher was a photograph from his youth, on one of his last tours.

It was horrendously faded, even at the time, but it showed my grandfather and three of his fellow soldiers standing with an African man and two small children who apparently weren't very interested in taking a photograph. One of the soldiers stood out due to his dark skin and varying print of uniform. The little boy wore an oversized sweatshirt that I assume was a gift from one of the Americans in the shot. Through the faded sepia-toned overexposure, it looked like it was a solid gray garment. The little girl next to him, looking more towards the camera (but not quite) was waving a small, rudimentary flag made of a solid black piece of cloth and a twig. I wonder if they're still alive.

My grandfather had his arm around the local man, a stark contrast between the natural dark skin of the decorated man and the pale demeanor of an American of European descent. My grandfather was shirtless, his jacket hanging folded off his shoulder, his pale skin eternally moments away from burning in the sun. You could see his circular scar, in the center of his chest. It looked like a wine-stain birthmark, in the light. I don't remember the story of its origin, but I am sure grandma had made one up somewhere along the way. They were probably in the foothills of one of the northern countries, because even for the era, the man looked like a tribal citizen. I know that he probably comingled with British forces, but no one else of modern outfit is visible in that photo. I really should try to find it sometime. It's in the rancher's small storage space with all of the other furnishings. I'm positive that the day I was first grown enough to look around my grandma's house on my own accord and had found this picture was the day she wove an on-the-spot fairy tale that I still find myself recounting.

"Oh, that was the time that Pop helped the witchdoctor patch a hole in his shabby roof…"

This world would be exponentially easier to bear were it possible to exist and actually survive in such a way. You know, take a tangible fact and paint it with ignorance, much like some media giants tend to do, although they do so in an unfortunately unpleasant manner. Stay naïve forever and achieve nirvana. "Oh, the world economies are imploding upon themselves? Let's pretend it's an extended vacation without pay." Dream-wash every fact, ignore every stabbing statistic, and make happy the memories of war.

It's funny the things you remember when you're just trying to shut it all out, to concentrate. Every layer, every detail, everything, gains this new film of significance when you're simply trying to hone in on a single event. All this, all of this personal lineage, all rapidly evolved, exploded rather, from the simple act of reaching for a bottle of bourbon that sat on top of my refrigerator. This fragment of a memory splintered off into the recollection of my grandmother giving me a fluffy, stuffed white elephant (or was it a manatee) with huge, black, adorable eyes when I had a particularly dreadful bought of night-terrors, due to a string of serial killings plaguing our country at the time. Every night, adolescent me would witness another murder in my sleep.

I assume my mother, the darling alcoholic, tried to maintain an air of class in her addiction, always choosing this particular (expensive) brand. Reaching for the bottle myself, staring at the label, I was assaulted by the memory of my grandmother and I sitting at a folding table in a backyard when I was younger, and then moving inside for dessert. A birthday party, my birthday party. I remember my father bringing in a cake, everyone smiling, and my mother discretely walking into the room and placing the large glass bottle on a desk at the side. Cake for those losing their teeth, bourbon for the middle adults. Immediately after placing the bottle, she raises a bulky camera, smiling, and takes a picture of the scene, blinding me back from history.

I'm an adult now, reaching for my own strain of addiction, yet find myself nostalgically taunted by the pink and orange flamenco dancer on the bottle. I find myself in the same single-story house, but this world is now without my beloved grandmother. Her life's work and home furnishings hidden away up a dangerous wooden ladder in the garage. My parents, I assume they're well, but we don't speak frequently. There was never a falling out; we simply live on two sides of the coin. Their (now) shared alcoholism lends itself to a lifestyle complemented by long weekend vacations in Vegas or road trips to seedy motels where I suspect they role-play in the bedroom. Hell, whatever it takes to keep a marriage together, I suppose. I'll never forget the summer before starting my graduate program, in which I found myself neglecting to adhere to the bold wisdom of the hat on the doorknob. So much leather. So, so much leather. At least they looked healthy. And far too happy.

I am not sure how these memories came to be. My grandfather, Africa, nostalgia, childhood birthday parties… Take note: something as innocent as reaching for an adult beverage results in conjuring images of your parents engaged in… physical manifestations of leather-based love. Don't start drinking. Or, if it's too late, drink more.

I grab the bottle and place it on the waist-level kitchen counter. I felt that I did not typically entertain, but my recent history was an indication of anything but antisocial attitudes. Jerry, Sara, and Ted are in the living room, huddled around a folding table (one that seems to follow me throughout my life) playing a half-assed game of cards. I return with glasses and the bottle and find Jerry anxiously glancing from the TV screen to his hand, as if he was seeking guidance.
"Relax, Jer," I pour the drink and he then seeks further wisdom from its depth. I turn to Ted.
"Thanks, man," Ted takes his glass and looks pleased with himself. He's probably decimating us all, as far as the game goes. Dominating… I think of my parents again.

I take a slow drink. Another.

A football game is on TV. I don't think either of the guys (and definitely not Sara) are particularly dedicated fans of the sport, but I think we silently reached the consensus that this is what men and their awkwardly-imposed girlfriend do when they are together outside of work. Sports, cards, and booze. Weren't vivacious and scantily-clad loose women supposed to be in this mix? That's what the beer commercials told us. Sara's wearing my sweatshirt that's too big for her thin frame: that's not scantily-clad. Not at all. Budweiser, you trifling cunts.

I do not remember the last time I used the television without company, I mean, actually used it for anything beyond ambience. Without the guys here, you know it doesn't interest me. I just needed some focused white-noise to drown out the silence. Men, we can sit in silence for hours having the time of our lives. But when each person is just as nervous as the next, as if we were all on some sort of twisted middle school blind date, the silence weighs on you like the millions of tons of ocean above a wreck. Perhaps that's why we considered each other friends. I mean, I hated them most days of the week, but we each shared that inability to really be comfortable with the other people in our lives, our other coworkers and neighbors. Perhaps that's how we found comfort.

Whenever Jerry's turn came around, the hand immediately developed an increased life-expectancy bleeding into the minutes. I don't know if it was a nervous-twitch sort of deal, but he would begin his turn, seemingly confident, and then retreat just as he began his action. It was like watching a bumbling elementary school student play checkers, extending his piece and rapidly retracting his movement, paranoid of what finality could bring and always keeping his clammy fingers clutched around the pieces, ensuring his longevity. It was enjoyable to watch Ted grow increasingly less patient during Jerry's turns. His frustration with his large friend became a point of humor in our circle. Personally, I took this moment to distract my thoughts away from the table. While Ted clenched his fist, bit his lip, brushed his black hair, smoothed out his shirt, or any combination of the lot, I lost myself by staring away from the card game at hand and looking at the television.

The football game was in its third quarter. The score was pretty close, but no one in attendance at my house had any loyalty to either of the colors. I couldn't tell you which team was from what major city in the United States without scrutinizing the acronyms, but I found distracted (and slightly inebriated) solace in the colors of either's uniform. One of the uniform's helmets depicted a simple logo of a warrior's spear jutting forward. Looking beyond my cards, my friends, and the television, I found my thoughts wandering back to my grandmother's house, this house we currently occupied, years ago.

This distraction bloomed from the warrior logo on the football helmet. Hell, it very well may have been in accordance to Native American symbolism, but in my personal history, this logo brought me back to my youth and the tales involving, yet again, my grandfather in Africa. The thoughts aroused from before (from the bottle of bourbon) suddenly found solid purchase in the recesses of my mind. As if these little symbols began locking together in a geared mechanism and were actually related. Oh, that's right: that African man's name was Billy. Well, that's at least what my grandpa and his group of Americans called him. I am sure that his name was really an indigenous and, honestly, more interesting name that a majority of the white men couldn't properly pronounce, thus they bastardized the poor young fellow to "Billy."

I hypothesize that he didn't really mind, for every picture I had seen of him and every story that grandma told of her husband's adventures seemed to depict him in a "brother-in-arms" archetype, so no bother. There, sitting in my living room, waiting for Jerry to fucking make a move or for Ted to snap and strangle Jerry (whichever happened first), I found myself tiptoeing through the years, thinking of a story that wove both my university years and my magical grandfather together.

Grandma told me this story one time, when I had pleaded for a "scary one," in which Pop and Billy (and their fellow soldiers) were terrorized by this creature that grandpa had called the "Toko-luck." When they were stationed and just hanging around camp, there wasn't so much to do in the arid climate, so they would prefer to stay spread out amongst the outpost, in the shade. However, at night, many of the units would consolidate towards one main portion of camp, a "town square," if you will, between the small city of canvas tents. They built a majestic American bonfire in its center and were complemented by a ring of large, generated light posts.

The Brits and the Americans, they were always either looking for a way to hook up with a local girl (not so much in these climates) or to frighten each other with horror stories from the field or from back home. In wartimes, this wasn't so difficult of a feat. I can tell from the sheer amount of European legends that grandma relayed to me that grandpa had a particular affinity for these stories and personal accounts. Lacking the previously mentioned supply of young women (or men, I don't judge) just yearning to be desecrated, these nightly campfires (when not being broken up by military exercises or enemy raids) were popular for hosting these bouts of storytelling between the men (boys, really).

Well, supposedly, one night, the Western world's adopted ally, Billy, had opted to tell a story. (Later research informed me that Billy was probably a native African from the southern region of the continent that had picked up a few of the European tongues that emanated from those taken colonies. I assume he was taken back to Europe on his own terms as a part of the military and worked as a sort of liaison between the military's arm and locals in campaigns.) The Brits and Americans had not had enough time to accrue many tales in their recent expedition so they were more than eager to hear whatever story Billy wanted to relay. I feel that I would have loved the man, through the subtle troublemaking spirit that Billy revealed through years of secondhand stories.

As all gathered around the sand-coated lounge, Billy started (in a thick native accent, I'm sure) about his time a thousand miles away, south, back "home". An insane old witchdoctor whom he respectably referred to as "his elder" was routinely charged with ridding neighboring villages of a particular specter that arose every so often. Through the retelling of my grandmother, Billy described to my grandfather and his friends a vile little creature that every inhabitant of the southern nations knew from childhood. This "toko-luck" was a wretched troll-like creature that essentially went around mucking up everyone's business. Billy told the men about the time one of these goblins gripped his village of birth in paranoia and fear.

Billy and his friends, who were all children when this reign began, remember not having to work in the crop or visit another elder for educational lessons (rudimentary math and tribal religion, I assume) for a week. I equate this halt in progress as the Western world's parallel to a snow day or gas leak in the public school's pipes. The children were pleased with their vacation, yet this manifested piece of folklore crippled and jammed a fork in the day-to-day of this village. Looking back with an adult eye, I smiled at these uneducated fools, but my high-and-mighty assertion was devastated one day, later, from my college years. Billy's story ended like your typical poltergeist-esque urban legend. The confirmation from a college professor made the story real to me, decades and continents away.

One of the general education requirements for completing my undergraduate degree demanded a social science elective. Not particularly interested in any topic within this vein, I offhandedly chose a political science course. The course was sub-par, but the professor was interesting enough. He was a thin, shorter white man with gray, shoulder-length novelist's hair, as if he was to be type-casted in a British spy film, assisting the main hero as a go-to source for information. Behind his silver-rimmed glasses, he spoke in a hand-waving demeanor, in an accent that baffled any and every associate and student of his.

Through years of playful teasing and taunting his students and colleagues with jeers of, "Well, guess where I'm from," and never adequately fulfilling the inquiry, we pieced together that he was from a European nation, forced into fleeing his home in one of the many cultural purges in its recent history, had settled in a south African nation for a short period of time, and then later Israel, until finally finding himself teaching in the States. His accent held a strong aura of Scottish or even Welsh hushes, whilst completely obliterating the pattern with seemingly random inflections. Regardless, it was this accent that confirmed some legitimacy to Billy's second-hand story, while simultaneously destroying my grandfather's pronunciation of the creature's name.

My professor had one day broken off on a stream of consciousness tangent that brought us to a day in his life during his tenure in South Africa. Having been exiled from his native European home, he must have had a colleague (having led a life of academia) who lived on the continent and knew of his plight. Well, the professor whose name was Mendilow, found his new residence directly across from the property of his trusted (and unnamed) associate. Perhaps the ease that Mendilow found in purchasing and moving into the property was an ominous precursor to this firsthand experience in local culture and lore.

Having its previous resident move out at an unheard rate of expedience, the professor found it necessary to employ a helping hand to rid his new home of some waste and uncollected belongings. He found no resistance in hiring a local woman, also unnamed in his recount, who was an efficient worker and a kind soul. She had a very young daughter who would sometimes (with Mendilow's inviting acceptance) spend the day with her mother as she tended the garden of the beautiful property. Life was simple and the days were long. Mendilow and his colleague neighbor conducted research and performed lectures for a salary at the nation's renowned liberal arts university and would spend the nights in the clutch of their shared yard, drinking fine spirits and discussing the world at large. However, one night, Mendilow's housemaid threw a wrench into the relaxation and surprising comfort of the new country that he now called home.

Without much warning, the assistant came bumbling out of his house with her supplies and belongings, scooped her daughter up, apologized, and left the property in a flurry of native curses and vulgarities. Mendilow and his neighbor were surprised and honestly, somewhat amused, by her frantic flight. He went into his home to find most of her daily chores finished, but his bedroom left untouched and still, quite messy. He hadn't yet moved his belongings into the room, as the previous inhabitant's lingering possessions were still strewn about. Mendilow retired to sleeping on the living room couch until his house was properly readied.

So, the search for help continued and a young man answered his call to arms. Like his previous employee, the work load was finished efficiently and with a smile, until the young man found himself in proximity to the master bedroom. Mendilow and his neighbor were once again in the garden discussing the quest for oil in the East when the assistant came out of the house in a hurry, preparing to apologize and leave the property, apparently for good. Mendilow saw this familiar panic on his face, but before he could react, his colleague rose from the cast-iron patio furniture and rushed to the boy. He could hear his colleague hushing and attempting to calm the boy and held him by each of his shoulders, demanding his attention and his glance.

After they talked for a few minutes and the state of emergency seemed to cool down, the young man approached Mendilow, shook his hand, and firmly apologized for having to relieve himself of any further employment. Without another word, the boy walked off into the setting day, to the village nearby. When his colleague returned to the table, Mendilow was justifiably concerned and confused. His colleague took a deep sip from his glass, looked off into the bush, then smirked and told Mendilow that his homestead contained a "tokolosh" and would need to be relieved of its presence before any local would even dare to think of helping him clean up his property, lest they draw the creature's attention to themselves. My professor was thoroughly dumbfounded at this discovery.

I could imagine him, this thick, slurring and shushing accent, "A... tokolaash?"

His colleague explained to him what the lore behind the creature was, the same explanation I could muster, and that they would need to consult a local holy man to rid the property of the being. Mendilow spent the following days scouring the room top-to-bottom, trying to discover this "creature." Eventually, he gave up, not knowing what the hell these locals could see in his house. Of course, reason and rationality made him laugh at this primitive fear, but after randomly screening multiple villagers about his house, an all-too-real fear began to creep into his daily life.

Eventually, he had a "professional" witchdoctor exorcise the entity and, surprisingly, all was well. He had alternatively hired both the young man and the mother to tend to his house's chores and they made no further comment concerning the diabolical gremlin that had (apparently) previously resided in his bedroom. To our class, he summed it up simply with, "when we deal with cultures and traditions not common to ours', we have to maintain an open mind and understand that not everything will immediately make sense to us," and he gave a laugh. "Hell, I still don't understand the whole thing involving the tokolosh. Your fellow man may appear to be just that (your fellow man), but who knows what burdens and beliefs he carries. He may not even know, himself. Sometimes you will not be able to explain the world around you. And sometimes, the world will not be able to explain why you do the things you do."

Rapidly returning from this light hearted memory and glancing down at the cards in my hands, then at Jerry still looking at his and thus inducing further rage from Ted, I couldn't help but agree. We are all strangers and people may never make any sense.
Sara and the guys were gone in a few more hours and I was still sitting in my empty living room, watching the highlights from the game. I lurched back in my chair, irritated away from the first-world, and stood to receive the phone ringing from the kitchen.

A house phone ringing is never good news. Your gut's typically right about these kinds of things.
Mine always is.

CHAPTER TWO
And my streak continues.

It was my supervisor. He said my name with a question mark at the end of it. I greeted him with a confused slur of vowels.
"Kevin… we need to have another talk,"
Within hours, I was sloshing through my house, knocking over furniture, yelling at the top of my lungs at whatever digital radio station I loaded on my computer. Mother fucker. California Dreaming by the Mamas and the Papas was pulsing through my house. I broke glasses. I broke lamps. I flipped a couch in my living room. I front-kicked my rolling office chair. Do you know that the singer of this band fucked his daughter? My heart pumped alcohol. The blood of Christ. I vomited in the kitchen. I was, apparently, one of those bad addicts who relapsed at the slightest hint of emotional trauma. If I was lucky, I would have my own show on MTV by the end of the year. Breaking glass. Lots of broken glass. That was my therapy.

At some point in my ordeal, Ted and or Jerry, may have learned of my most recent bout of inebriation due to my cellular phone becoming my weapon of choice in these crusades. I must have redialed my supervisor's personal number a dozen times. Before tonight, I never had a reason to call the schmuck. Tonight was different. He needed to sing alongside me. And, I suppose, vomit alongside me. After dozens of calls to strangers and friends, each as reliable as the other, the fat fuck Jerry arrived at my house, knocking at the door. I was almost naked when I responded to his fists banging against the house's siding: "No, Jerry, I'm fine! Just fucking peachy… do you want to come in?"

When I opened the door, the poor guy looked genuinely worried. When he opened the storm door and reached out towards me, I spat on his fat paws. "No, Jerry. I'm celebrating my freedom."

The company I had worked for had gone under.

I was, again, unemployed.

When I recalled this fact, you know, the reason for my "celebration," I suddenly missed my old co-worker, Walter Hale, greatly. Jerry slid through the front door and came rushing to my side. I was on my knees, bawling.

"Why, Walt, you old fuck?! Why?!"

"Kevin… Kevin, calm down… it'll be… it'll be okay, man," Jerry tried to pull me to my feet from under my armpits.

"No, Jerry – Walt's dead! He's not coming back!"

"Is that why you're so upset?" he asked, earnestly. "Is that why you're drunk dialing half of your phone's contacts? … Who's Walt?"

"Oh…" I realized the overwhelming asymmetrical disparity of information present. "No. I'm out of a job again. The company went under."

I began sobbing. I guess the minute nature of this revelation surprised Jerry.

"Oh," he said. "I see. Listen, man. You'll be fine. I'll talk to the boss on Monday. I'll tell him you'll be more cheerful. You could easily get your old job back. We could probably get some sort of health reason from a doctor or something. You were easily one of our better programmers—"

Images of the fat Swedish programmer flashed through my mind: visions of him at the coffee machine, of him on the blow-up exercise ball, of him on the campus mall, on a Segway scooter, washing his hands in the company restroom – "No. Fuck that noise, Jerry. Fuck that Swedish fuck."

"Kevin… what? Kevin, calm down. You're drunk. You really need to just rest for a bit."

I punched Jerry. A decent haymaker punch. I really should have been a fighter. You know, except for that whole lanky frame thing.

He rubbed his chin for a moment, looked at me, startled, his curly hair bouncing with each glance he shot me. "You're beyond help, Kevin," and began tearing up. He turned and left.

I stumbled to my computer. I cranked the volume on my speakers and let the music flow through my house. Returning to my living room, I thought for a moment that it would have been a tidier scene if I had performed a five-minute, at-home abortion instead, primarily utilizing wire hangers and small flights of stairs. One of my only two living friends was long gone and the other was probably not going to show up, per Jerry's warning. My own vomit, constituting of not-much-more than my unfiltered bile and the bits of undigested food that had managed to hide in the recesses of my tract from yesterday morning, coated the carpet, the ceiling, the wall, my clothes. There may have been some blood in that delightful brew. Yes, there was absolutely blood in there. This discovery caused me to halt my drunken romp for a moment, but then that lacking sweep of rationality hit me and I continued my tirade.

My thoughts should have been, "I should probably call an ambulance."
My thoughts actually were, "How many more shots until Jay Leno's chin was fuckable?"

The television was on. The music was still pounding. I felt as if the walls were crawling with the shards of broken glass, somehow animated into sentient, breathing creatures destined to torment me in my blazed stupor. Said glass-beetles chattered in this crescendo of buzzing that resembled those late August cicadas. Organically-produced white noise.
"Stop it!" I shouted and clawed at the ceiling fan. One of my swinging fists broke the glass cover of the lighting and I felt the warm trickle of blood immediately dance down my forearm. I stared at the injury in silence for a moment and grunted in a stupid little laugh.

Once more, I decided that I needed to have a chat with my old supervisor. You know, just for closure's sake. I rang him on my cell. Dull buzzing. Dull buzzing. No one picked up. No bother, I probably couldn't hear him over the shrill cries of the Glass Beetles anyway. Walking on my knees towards the kitchen, I swept my car keys off the countertop. The business card he presented me when we first had met included his mailing address, which was noticeably lacking a "P.O. Box" in front of it, so I assumed it to be his residence. I thought that I should pay him a visit.

I had somehow managed to get out of my house (definitely leaving my front door open, my house blaring music into the dark night) and behind the wheel of my car. The Tokolosh waved "Goodbye!" from the threshold of the doorway. I roughly recognized the name of the street my supervisor lived on and my car began rolling down the driveway with a decimated me behind the wheel. Picking up precisely where I had left off inside, I selected a soundtrack for my journey on the radio and nearly drove my eardrums to hemorrhaging, accelerating down the residential thoroughfare.

It wouldn't have taken me more than fifteen minutes on a non-inebriated license, but hey, what can you do? I left my neighborhood and crept onto the county highway. He lived just over the Old Iron Bridge (located on the aptly named "Ironbridge Road"), which spanned Phillips' Creek. Narrowly avoiding an old man walking his dog (on the sidewalk) I took the turn onto the rural highroad. Seriously, who would be walking their dog when it was this dark out? Please. Somewhere in the deepest trenches of my mind, a stray bit of meaning attached itself to a dim flashing that kept catching my eye. There: in the rearview mirror of my car, about half a mile behind me on the county road, a police cruiser was now in pursuit. Ah. Perhaps taking that sidewalk just a bit too fast (or, at all) sold me out.

Well, I was fucked anyway. It's funny, watching those Joe Blows on COPS get torn out of their disabled vehicles, filthy, drunken white-trash, yelling at the police officer... you never even think that that could be you. You never imagine that you'll be the one throwing racial slurs at the Caucasian police officer, drunk off your ass, running away in a palsy-laden jaunt. I grasped at the front of my shirt and felt the warm, wet bile from my insides, smelled the sickening aroma of my body odor, and giggled, my voice sounding horrendously out of tune: yeah, you never think that that could be you, until you're on the cusp of making, yet another, poor decision.

My car delicately disregarded the painted lines designating the center of the narrowing road that evolved into the iron bridge. My inebriated conscious delicately disregarded the increasingly-annoying blare of the sirens closing in behind me. My vehicle's front-end delicately disregarded the guardrail of the decaying bridge as my careless maneuvering sent me over the edge. Everything slows down when you're in freefall. Yes, just like the movies.

A discarded to-go cup from a local fast food place exploded in its cup-holder. I was showered in day-old, warm and flat soda and hiccupped a thin layer of spittle in amused surprise. Reacting, I raised my arms and braced myself against the roof of my plummeting car. In the rapidly-firing shots of memories flooding my vision, I realized that in all my years in this small town, I had never once dipped my foot into Phillips' Creek. I assumed, logically, that that was about to change. My vision began to blur further. I guess that my body had finally begun to absorb those last bits of going-away drink I stole before I had left my house. Just as things were getting good.

The car slammed into the creek under the bridge and I watched myself break my nose against the steering wheel. Ah, reliable old ironsides, Oliver Wendell Holmes be damned: no airbags were deployed. Booze and blood stole my vision and I guess my body felt that now, in this sinking vehicle, was an ideal time to rest. White and yellow light flashed and flitted across my dashboard as the water bubbled around. I caught glimpses of the known red-and-blue over the edge of the bridge where I had crashed through. As my vessel sank at a surprising pace, visions of portly European career-thieves and my dearest Walt drifted through the dark water. In addition to these personal icons, I could have sworn I also saw an obscenely-large creature, painted a hazy gray or off-white, loll past me. Probably, no, definitely, a distant cousin to the Glass Beetles laying claim to my home as I sank. The Tokolosh from my childhood rode the amphibious-elephant like a horse and cackled like a hyena, taunting my failing nervous system.

It is at this point in my story that we have almost caught up to the current hour. It is at this point that I am no longer painting you a picture of the past.

I woke up before I opened my eyes. There weren't any monitors beeping, or nurses shuffling around: I wasn't in a hospital. Slowly opening my heavy eyes, I learned that I was in my own room, at home. Upon this realization, I quickly sat up, and instantly dropped back, suddenly aware of the weight of my upper body.

"Oh, my," I closed my eyes and turned into my pillow. After exhaling, I attempted to sit up once more. Braced for the weakness of my muscles, I managed to sit up, leaning back on both arms. It seemed as if I was evading the police mere hours ago. I glanced at my digital alarm clock: 3.24 pm. Well, there goes a productive day.

I noticed a neat stack of papers on top of a folder on my nightstand. My vision still blurred occasionally, so without even the most heartless of attempts, my head processed these documents as medical receipts, prescriptions, and instructions. How very exciting. I could feel the stack weigh towards the bottom as I hefted it in my hands. Inevitably, court summons and infinite fines from the police department sat in the trenches of the bureaucracy. None of these really seemed important to me at the moment.

I found some comforting familiarity on the premiere cover sheet of one of the medical bundles. A bright orange prescription bottle holds a handful of light blue pills, comfortably sitting in a pocket of residual blue-white powder. I do not recognize the name of the medicine. A bright neon pink sticky note was pasted to the upper left hand corner of one of my medicinal instructions and it informed me that "fresh groceries were in the refrigerator" and that it had "been a pleasure taking care of you, Kevin," signed with a quaint, potentially handicapped, smiley face. Oh, it appears that I had accrued caregivers in my blitzed state. I rose from my bed, replacing the papers on the piece of furniture.

I changed into a pair of plaid pajama bottoms and slowly shuffled into my kitchen. I saw a large brown paper bag (enveloped in a supportive plastic bag) balancing on the center of my table. I inferred that these were the dry goods and some "fresh" groceries were also being climate-controlled in my fridge. I stumbled to sit at my table and mulled through the paper bag. I inaccurately tore a box of granola bars open and began chewing on one. They were decently stale. I hadn't realized how hungry I had been. I had to rotate the box of the granola bars; the torn smile of the Quaker man didn't sit well with me in my cautious demeanor. I was a recovering patient, mind you.

An old newspaper sat on one of the chairs at the table, undoubtedly a relic from my caregiver's existence here. Unfortunately, the sentimentality of the gift was lost as my jaw dropped and I sprinkled the cover with bits of moist granola and processed chocolate chips. A fresher print of the Times sat on the table and I moved to stack them, to start cleaning up my house, and I realized something striking between these two copies: the newspaper had subtlety informed me that two months had passed since my binge.

CHAPTER THREE

I began to cry. Not emotionally, not as a depressive reaction, but hey, it was happening. Tears were rolling out of my widened eyes as I stared at the date. How in the hell did this happen? I mean, I guess it made sense why I wasn't in the hospital and instead receiving home-care – no way would I have been home so shortly after my accident had it really only been last night. I was stricken with an incredible sense of syncope.

Bracing against the kitchen table, I slowly lowered my head onto my folded arms. Slow, even, breaths. Alright. No big deal. I have been out of it for two months. I began to notice the small bits of my previous life emanating from around my kitchen, specters from another existence. Get-Well-Soon cards, primarily from Jerry and Ted, flowers from my old employers, advertisements delivered by the mailman, a letter from Sara: they all haunted me from my place in the center of the room.

I had been unconscious for nearly two months and all I wanted to do was sleep. Sleep until things made sense again. Rest until I was actually a part of the present, not a visitor in some time-delayed immigration struggling to adapt to this unknown modern society. I am so fucking pathetic. Just imagine my displacement if I was actually a social being, imagine if I had a social circle to catch up with. Hell, I should have just blasted my brains out right then and there. But, for the moment, in this swirling world of uncertainty, I felt just a second's relief of comfort in this new sanctity of anonymity.

I walked into my small office and felt compelled to turn on the computer. I really wasn't up to the task, apparently, as I kept strolling through the room and into the living room. I sank into the recliner and looked out of my front windows. It was a mild, relatively sunny day outside and the thickening layers of clouds kept the sun from scorching the tired earth. An older man glided by on a bicycle without looking up, not that he would have noticed me to begin with. I grabbed the wooden knob on the side of the chair and pressed myself back, extending the chair's footrest. With my neck awkwardly craning up and backwards, I closed my eyes and willed myself to sleep for a few hours.

I had to get something started when I woke up.

Not even twelve hours in and this lackadaisical lifestyle was already boring holes into my sanity. I walked back into my office, forced myself onto the computer, and tried to catch myself up with whatever I had missed in the previous two months, whatever would have concerned me. Hobbies. Interests. You know, people things.

A new Linux distro was due any day now; the town was expecting torrential downpours tonight; an author that I mildly enjoyed in high school was releasing a new book soon (but I hadn't read him for years at this point); a few relevant job openings had appeared in my vicinity. I didn't feel up to it. It was like getting over an emotional break up, that is, looking for a new job after losing Walt. I've been unawake for days at a time, and I hadn't pondered his death, at least to my memory. It was a fresh wound again. Sure, weeks had passed since it happened, but when you cut out more than half of the time due to what you assume is a comatose condition, does it really count as a healthy grieving period?

Momentarily lapsing into my spirited (pun intended) ways, I grabbed a large bottle of vodka and took it to my bedroom, like a child with his stuffed bear. However, not a drop was consumed. I lay awake, cradling that damn bottle like a baby, staring out my window, curtains drawn. A gentle rain had settled in around ten pm and would continue to grow in strength well into tomorrow morning. I barely slept at all. I laid in bed through the early hours of the day, watching the sun's journey across the sky, until it was dark, once again. Hunger had yet to make a return appearance. I was an android. I barely existed on this side of being.

I needed physical release. I, of all people, felt the need to go out and, hell, socialize.

Meeting people in bars was always an adventure. It was never a go al, it was always a residual effect. It was always detritus of the rare night out with coworkers. Considering my hefty account at the regional hospital, I can't really tout these lustful binges as anything beyond a poor decision. You could almost compare these "dates" as an addict dating his dealer; a doctor, his patient. I like to believe that "truck driver fucking his truck," (i.e., acting as a destroyer of things that adequately maintained him) was a more suitable, and even whimsical, approach at classification. Take your pick, artist.

It was almost like a buffet on most nights. Simply substitute "food" with sad people. I mean, the town wasn't that populated and the women typically held their liquor as successfully as they had held their (non-existent) standards. Some nights, the selection was premium. You could even hold a conversation with some of the bar's patrons. However, so long as we're sticking to the "buffet" metaphor, some nights were the class-equivalent of a Sizzler opened for business long after their heated-trays and vats were disabled. The women (and the men in attendance, for that matter) were those vile reminders of whatever their former glories held (chowder, steak, whatever you could pour into a warmed vat) pathetically and disgustingly clinging to the metallic walls that formed their world.

My favorites, easily, were those college-aged sweethearts that somehow found themselves drinking to loneliness in a low-key bar on the far side of town. It was usually some sob-story involving being stood up by some frat boy, or losing a job or loved one, or just not feeling "like they fit in." Believe me, it was all very enlightening. It amazes me that the younger portion of our generation loves, so desperately, to believe and bemoan the very fact that they simply don't belong and demand that they must exist as an enigma to the world. If all of these like-minded refugees banded together, hell, they'd realized that their tragic tale of solidarity is just the same as everyone else's. A cookie-cutter tragedy in which every player feels unique.

I needed relief. I hadn't gone out to one of these establishments since long before my accident, long before I lost my initial job, long before the fat Swede ruined my life. A few minutes sober, I deserved such a treat.

The young bartender was cheerful. There weren't many other customers this early. They would probably begin filtering in around eight pm. She wore a bit too much makeup and was a tad on the heavy side. I told her what I wanted and diffused her small talk. What an absolute pain in the ass it was to bear such charmingly good looks when everyone else existed simply as a means.

A little bit of life passed. I sketched interface designs on the napkin in front me, my auxiliary napkin, the one not cushioning my glass. Every so often, I sat up and swept the bar, looking for tonight's therapist. I had almost given up when I noticed her. Ah, there she was. There, in the corner, a young redhead (probably a junior at the university) sat at a table with obnoxiously tall chairs, cradling her cell phone, somber in its pale glow.

I nodded at the bartender and shot my thumb in the direction of the redhead. She scrunched her nose and nodded back. Stupid bitch. I guess she felt like we had made a connection or what have you. Nope. I sidled over to the girl's table and introduced myself.

"Hello there," I extended my hand. She sniffed and looked up.

"Hi," she meekly replied.

"I'm Jonathan," I said, comfortable in the fact that my name is Kevin.

"Hello, Jon," she whimpered, looking at her phone.

"What's the problem?"

Boyfriend? Exams? Roommates?

"I don't know. This guy I've been seeing stood me up tonight. He's out with fucking Sherry. Sherry. This week wasn't good, either. Pretty sure I'm failing. And the girls at the house have been so incredibly bitchy lately." Man, am I fucking good or what.

"That's a real shame."

I made a mock-pout and sat down.

Throughout the rest of the night, we "hit it off."

I don't remember her name. I wasn't overly drunk or anything of that nature, she was just very forgettable. Some sad people usually are. We went back to her shared townhouse. Apparently, she was a part of some sorority, but many of her sisters were out that night (apparently at the same function as Fucking Sherry and this one's presumably ex-boyfriend) so the trip to her bedroom was relatively uneventful.

"One second… Jonathan…" she slurred and stumbled towards her bathroom, leaving me on her bed, sitting up on my elbows. I heard water running and her shuffling around behind the bathroom door, washing, touching up her makeup, etc.

"Hello," a voice gave me a start from the doorway. One of her roommates, a dark-skinned girl with incredible curves eyed me, leaning on the frame of the door.

"Hi there," I chirped. She looked me up and down, apparently not impressed.

"You're a bit older than the guys Meg's usually into…?" I couldn't tell if she was telling me or asking me to explain the scenario.

"Well… aren't I the lucky one?" I smiled, and if I had a drink in my hand, I would have raised it to her in a mock-toast.

"Hmph," she agreed, apparently not up to a battle of wits. "Have fun."

She crossed into the room and banged twice on the bathroom door, hard, "Hey, Meg, we're all back. If you need anything, I'll be across the hall." The redhead, whose name was Meg, thanked her behind a wooden door and mouthful of toothpaste.

"Goodnight," the girl nodded towards me as she left. I stared after her as she closed the door.

The bathroom door opened and the light clicked off. Meg stood in its threshold in an expensive pair of underwear, trying to look seductive under a veil of inebriation. She locked her bedroom door, turned off the other light, and I could hear her small feet pat across the room towards me. My heartbeat increased. The mourning girl fell onto me, a bit heavier than intended, and began to sloppily kiss at my chin, at my neck, anywhere but my mouth it seemed, and was slobbering everywhere. Some poor freshman schmuck would probably have found this incredibly attractive; I was simply getting past the slow part.

After she descended my body, unbuttoned my shirt and unzipped my pants, she began to show heavier signs of drunkenness than I had previously planned for. Oh, dear. Her movements became stilted and the grace she tried to display in the actions of her lips was clumsy and lopsided. I didn't know there could be an unsatisfactory oral experience, but this slurring mess was beginning to prove me wrong.

"Honey, wait a second," I lifted the redheaded-deadweight away from her assumed duty and laid her back where I had been laying. The least I could do was provide some whimsy where she had failed. She didn't object. She was not as elegant of a person who you'd take home to show the parents. At least I didn't think so. She was by no means "dirty," but hell, she was in college. I couldn't have asked for too much. I'm the bad guy here. What would my grandmother think. Great, thinking of grandmothers now. "Jonathan…" she sighed.
I stopped for a moment. Through a mouthful I spat, "Who the fuck is Jonathan?" and then I remembered.
She almost sat up on her elbows, "What?…" I lowered my head and told her to shut up. She complied.

After a while, it seems like we both had lost ourselves. I was preoccupied in my thoughts, weighing what would happen if I married this girl, what our kids would look like, where she would work, if she would accept my alcoholism. Of course, these were all the fleeting thoughts of oral sex and I would never seriously contemplate such inept commitments on such a short span of time. That would be lunacy.

I continued and my thoughts continued to drift. Over the years, I've occasionally found myself imagining what some people thought of when they performed the act. It wasn't particularly taxing on the provider, but I know that for many, it was simply a game of "when is it my turn?" Could you imagine a boy in high school, used to the instant-gratification bestowed by the modern world and, hell, video games? Five minutes would exist as an eternity to the poor brat. His girlfriend would be disappointed and then they'd go watch a movie, and he'd be up for it and she'd die a little on the inside and he'd be confused and devastated when she's off blowing the next 'schmo. The circle of life, again: give, get, wipe off your face, and onto the next responsibility.

Minutes ticked by and I lost track of the work at hand. Of course, I was still in this girl's dorm room, doing the Lord's work, but up there, mentally, I was elsewhere. Time disappeared and I felt oddly top-heavy, as if I didn't have a body, but no, I felt as though I was actually standing. It was a semi-conscious dream, that's all.

I was in a clearing in a darkened wood. Purple shadows and granite-shaded ash were caught in gentle pockets of swirling wind and the sky burned with varying tones of bright blue, white, and red, blending in with the purple aura of this universe. This was by no means frightening; the whole thing was very relaxing, beautiful, and I was in control. There were others there, but I couldn't really get a decent look at them. As if their existence was in direct accord to my own (the lack of a body, but the knowledge of one's own presence), I couldn't see them, but they were definitely there. They were allies. Perhaps not amiable hosts or friends, but each positively relishing in the collective anticipation of the moment. I crouched next to the bark of a thick, tall tree. The tree was ashen and black in color, adhering to the color scheme of this vision. I brushed my fingers along the bottom of the bark and raised my hand to my eyes. The world occasionally burst with bright light and over-exposed blinding flashes of photography saturation.

My point of view became heavily pixilated, as if I were in some old video game from the eighties. I took the dark purple ash that had pooled at the base of the tree and I smeared it under my eyes, along my jaw, on my neck. They were practiced motions in an alphabet unbeknownst to me, but a language my avatar was apparently quite fluent in.

There was a constant chatter of casual, excited conversation and some familiar, acoustic music drifted in through the amaranthine forest, as if we were all waiting for a play or a movie in a theatre. A dull rumbling began, there, somewhere in front of me, of us, hundreds of feet in the distance. It wasn't frightening and it did not threaten our gathering, but a hush quickly fell upon my group. I did not know what this meant, as an observer looking in, but I felt a sharp sense of joy and enthusiasm sweep my player. I dropped my arms, palms forward, and took a deep breath in. The group's guest was arriving. There, the trees were gently parting. I was momentarily broken from this trance-like state and torn from the immersion of this universe: the large white floating elephant, more like a manatee, from my childhood was there, its front legs paw-like and its trunk short and wide, unlike the elephants I knew from the zoo and on the Discovery Channel. His usual creamy texture was still there, but now bore streaks of purple, red-clay, and black ash from this alternate world I found myself looking in on.

The unseen crowd around me burst in excitement, in applause, and the trees further broke down around the gigantic, slow-moving creature as he lowered in from his hover, ready to make a gentle landfall. His large, bulbous eyes slowly swept the scene, invisible black spheres under the iridescent lenses. It's easy to love this creature, to think he's "cute" – but my avatar seems to distantly recall a hidden truth of potential rage and devastation within the creature's whim and ability. This makes me, real me, want to turn and run, but my player simply raises his arms towards the beast. I feel myself smile. If it were possible for the large, cream-colored alien to smile, I'm sure that's what it would be doing. I could hear its voice, distant and non-existent, amplified only in my mind: Hello, Kevin. It is time.

I'm back in the dorm room. The girl is climaxing and I hold onto her legs, her hips, acting involved, excited, turned on. She twists and convulses and then collapses, dead, satisfied, and mewing as she stretches her back, her legs, her body. I hold her for a moment, and she twitches into an awkward flash of activity, about to start a conversation. She then giggles, and she falls asleep, still drunk from the night. I'm not let down. My arms are cradling the unconscious stranger and I'm staring up at the ceiling, trying to piece together what all of that just meant.

"So, you got high off of some college girl's snatch?" Oh dear Sara was such a dainty flower, so pleasant and worldly.
"More or less. It was bizarre."
"I'd fucking say. You saw retro-nerd Valhalla while going down on a drunk girl. Cheers to you, Kevin,"
Sara tilted her bottle of soda my way and took a drink. Sara was terribly thin and diabetic. I watched the muscles of her throat contract and pulse with each swallow. A fraction of the bottle's forty grams of sugar disappeared with each mouthful and I wondered if she was drinking the stuff because she felt lightheaded. You know, low blood sugar, the whole nine. I knew that she felt my gaze, but she kept her stare towards the television after her drink.
"Are you alright?" I asked her, sincerely. Honestly.
"Yeah, Kevin. I'm fine." She then busied herself with her cellphone.

We weren't a couple. God damn it, Sara. You know this and you set these terms yourself. Live with your fucking choice. You see, Sara and I have known each other for years. I would never leave Deptford County and Sara had no choice but to stay. She was that failed actress type, the one who never actively sought an audition, but still felt oppressed. Regardless, she was my one constant, my female Jerry and Ted. When I got my first post-graduation job, she reamed me for not moving closer to the company's campus, claiming that it was "my big chance at escaping Deptford" – I didn't really care. I liked the drive on most days. Her and the guys became friends at some point, probably an incident of Sara inviting herself over during one of our half-hearted games of poker.

She's always been there, throughout the handful of un-spirited "relationships" I've experienced and I've always been there for her, watching her date scumbag after scumbag of Deptford's finest. But, as you know, I've been in a romantic drought since high school (due to other circumstances) and she's not willing to marry any of the dregs that we grew up with that still dwell these parts. So, naturally, we let ourselves go on occasion, getting blitzed and making poor decisions within the confines of a bedroom. For her, I assumed it was to merely quench that human desire to be wanted, and for dear old Kevin, it was a means to ensure the avoidance of an over-accumulation of testosterone that inevitably results in a random shooting of the local post office or shopping mall. The closest thing to love we'd ever have.
"Sorry," I frowned.
"Not a problem, dear," she half-smiled.
I would not feel guilty. She, whether purposely or not, had fucked with my fleeting emotions enough over the years. For every failed rock star schmuck that she blew before coming over my house to emotionally break down, a drunken mess, for every time she failed to pick me up at the bus station, for every et cetera of failed friendship responsibilities, I could know no shame in her presence and I refused to bear it now.

CHAPTER FOUR

Sara spent the night with me. After all, I was fresh from my apparent coma and in dire need of a friend.

She knew me well: she made no mention of my accident. It was as if I had never "left". She slept, curled against me, one of my arms under her, and the other, wrapped around, locked at her waist, like a normal couple would. She purred quietly in her deep sleep and I could sense her unconscious smile in my bedroom. Her blonde hair frayed from the pillow and gently covered some of my face when I tried to nuzzle in and get some sleep. That sweet solace would not yet greet me, so I was only in momentary bewilderment at the scent of her, of Sara.

With her hair no longer needing to adhere to gravity, I could see a bit of her thin neck. Her pale skin glowed in the calm blue of my room at night and I saw, for the first time in quite a while, an old, pleasant picture. Two incredibly cartoonish elephants have their trunks clasped, facing each other, with a small cloud of bright red hearts floating away from their touch. The pastel green elephant on the left is the male and the light pink one on the right is his mate. They're each no larger than a quarter and the tattoo really is quite precious. I believe this was a small doodle Sara had drawn as far back as elementary school, if I recall. She had the ink done the senior year of high school, not purposing it as a symbol of defiance, but as a token of innocent love. I stupidly wonder if she remembers if it's still there, the tiny drawing on the back of her neck. This thought comforts me, these thoughts of a young Sara. Days when I was preoccupied with a devastating Mariah. Pastel elephants in an Eskimo-kiss. Day dreams. Sara. I'm asleep.

I'm in the woods.

They're not in the least bit magical or beautiful. The late autumn climate had destroyed much of the former green glory and the world has exploded in gray, brown, and orange, but it is night. Everything has an extra layer of black. The trees are tall, thin, and dead or dying. The world is quiet and the air is still. I am completely aware of myself, although I feel like a stranger in this place. Leaves kick up. A girl, seemingly only a few years my junior, runs past me, oblivious of my presence. Alas, I am a mere spectator here. I glance in her wake and see a dark figure moving from the far end of the path. I feel a tinge of panic and turn towards the fleeing girl and follow her quickly. I am not a target in this universe, but I am worried for the girl.

The world shifts and I am now in front of the girl, as if the world determined that I had not need waste my time chasing her and wanted me to simply cut to the point. The pursuing figure quickly catches up to the girl and clumsily drags her to the ground, laden in dead, dirty leaves. He flips her onto her back and straddles her, holding her down with all of his weight. Time begins to crawl. The girl really is beautiful. In my younger days, she would have been my end-all knockout. She had jet black hair, accented with streaks of purple that were only noticeable when she caught it in the dead moonlight, as she twisted and attempted to jerk her way out from under her attacker. Her skin was incredibly fair, another artistically beautiful yet useless feature of this terrible scene unfolding before my eyes.

For a moment, I feel as if she looks past the attacker on top of her and locks me in a shocked gaze. I sense familiarity in her dying stare. This is unfortunate whimsy, as time hastens again and the assault proceeds without any possible intervention on my behalf. I can now tell that the person on top of her is obviously a man, although his face is concealed by the synthetic darkness of my dream. A charcoal gray hooded sweatshirt is drawn over his head, and an expensive-looking black duster jacket cloaks the rest of his body. Silently, quickly, a large hunting knife is tossed to his assistance from among the shadows. I wince at the audible moment of entry as the girl lets out a startled whimper upon the stab. I only now realize that she had not been screaming or shrieking during the entire hysterical takedown. The man sits back, on the girl's thighs, and I hear him grunt in satisfaction, his voice raspy and broken.

I attempt, repeatedly, futilely, to kick the man off of her, but I am a ghost here. I could do nothing to change what I have just witnessed. After a few moments of resting, like a hunter after a prize shot, the man in the duster starts to work on his kill. After pulling the hunting knife from her chest, he wipes it on his jacket and reuses it to cut cleanly down the center of her dark purple thermal shirt. I feel incredibly dirty watching this, as he shows her stomach and black bra to the world. He further cuts the black underwear from the center and she is lying there, completely exposed, her chest and the contours of her body pure even after being contaminated by death. Besides the stab wound gently fissuring crimson black blood, she is an image of beauty. The son of a bitch on top of her laughs throatily and smears the dark blood over the white of her skin. I again attempt to cease this desecration, but it is useless. He's whispering something intangible and I move closer to try to understand. As I get mere inches away from his concealed mouth (still looking away from my beloved victim), he stops. He looks up and he somehow senses my presence. A horn blares in the distance. I'm awake.

Sara reaches to turn off the alarm clock on the end table, which was synchronized with the blast in my dream. I realize that I'm cold and sweating. My hands are visibly shaking. Of course she notices.

"Kevin, what's the matter?" she flicks on the light and sits up, stroking the hair behind my ear, instantly taking care of me. Although sick to my stomach and anxious to see the conclusion of that macabre film, I already feel a bit better. I'm shirtless, per my typical sleeping custom. She gingerly traces down my chest. She's being purely comforting, but I feel an all-too-human burst of warmth somewhere in my mind.

"Just a nightmare. Just like when I was little," I give a dead laugh.

"People dying?"

"Always," I confirmed and smiled. "Oh well."

"Well, as long as you're alright, Kevin," she looks at the clock. "Did you screw with this?"

I shake my head and shrug. I leaned back and drew the sheets to me once more. Sara turned out the light, annoyed by the freak presence of the alarm clock (which had uselessly exploded to life at three in the morning) and tried to get comfortable again. But that spark she ignited in me refused to die and a terrible thought lingered and festered and eventually manifested in that relationship-borne cancer that set ships to sea and men, good and bad alike, to war. We, once again, confirmed exactly why men and women of comparable attraction cannot simply remain Platonic friends given a long enough period of cohabitation. It was stupid of me to perpetuate, stupid of me to initiate. It was a purely physical instinct that started it and I felt emotionally drained halfway through the mess. Time went by. She was on top of me. Her hands were on my chest. She must have noticed a change in my expression and stopped grinding her hips into me.

"Kevin. What's. Wrong." she stayed right there.

I didn't know how to react. I lack social finesse.

"A dead girl," I answered honestly.

"Okay…" she looked away, embarrassed, confused, worried, and got off of me. She lay on her side, away from me, and apologized for even starting it tonight. I assured her not to feel sorry, "it was my fault," etc. and pulled her towards me, resuming our initial, locked-in position. This consoled her, although it was originally me who needed the care, and we both eventually passed out, confused by what had just unfolded.

The dead girl still haunted my thoughts.

CHAPTER FIVE

Ted, Jerry, Sara, and I went to breakfast the next morning.

I busied myself reading the newspaper that some kind soul had left after finishing before me. We were in a small booth at a restaurant that prides itself as your typical American diner. There were hundreds, thousands even, across the country. Yes, you've been there. No, it wasn't anything spectacular. But we were there. Jerry was having an animated back-and-fourth with the waitress determining exactly what was contained in his whimsically titled breakfast platter. The process of taking the rest of the table's orders was far less exciting (and thus, much more rapid). After Jerry and the waitress were finished reciting what amounted to, as far as time is concerned, a verbal rendition of Paradise Lost, I sat back and closed my eyes for a moment. Surprisingly, after a quiet night of restless turning and remaining half-sleep next to Sara, I found myself at ease, comfortable, enjoying myself alongside my weary-eyed friends.

The emotionally driven spite and unintentional verbal lashings that I had laid upon them, surrounding my inebriated incident, were in the past, and we were trying to move past them as a group. They, noticeably, had not pressed further concerning my status and lack of employment. I bore a sleepy conscious.

Of course, the dead girl was still there, just outside my line of vision, outside my train of thought, always peeking in, always there. She would be sitting at the diner's breakfast counter and then go. The waitress would ask us if we needed anything and for a moment, it was her. But these were all just the tired bursts of hallucinations. I could tell last night's incident had shaken Sara. I've been far from an easy person to be around recently, but I've hadn't had such organic episodes in years. My adult tantrums are typically induced by chemicals, but you know that by now.

The food came and we ate. Quiet conversation and a content mood prevailed.

Ted pointed to the newspaper that I had folded once and tucked under my plate. We were all nearly finished and I guess Ted searched for something to occupy his thoughts, having born a barren plate.

"Kevin," he said, still pointing. "Jerry's never been to a Deptford fair, huh?"

He moved to take a sip from his glass of water. I thought this over for a second.

"Huh. I guess not," and I couldn't help but smile a bit. Having grown up in Deptford County, the annual county fair was no big deal to me. It was just another yearly ritual, like our non-religious celebrations of Christmas and Easter, or kids going out on Halloween. Between Spring and Summer, Deptford's finest came out to mingle at the weekend long county fair. 4-H clubs hosted pens and tents where miserable animals would bemoan the graceless handling of young children and the mentally handicapped and senior citizens would dance and subsequently pass out due to dehydration at the hardwood dance floor, under the drunken crooning of the hired Frank Sinatra impersonator.

"Is it any good?" Jerry asked, bacon grease coating his chin.

"It's nothing new," Ted shrugged. "Just your typical county fair, you know?"

"Hm," Jerry nodded. "I'd go if you guys wanted to. But," he pointed at the newspaper. "What's that thing?"

At the top of the article advertising the fair was a small logo that the county embraced as an emblem of sorts, as if we were a sports team. A rough doodle of a bulbous creature sat just behind the capital print of DEPTFORD COUNTY and its subscript of Annual County Fair. Jerry, of course, was asking what the doodle was supposed to represent. Having grown up in the area, Ted and I instantly recognized our beloved "Lenny," but he probably looked a tad goofy to our outsider friend. Sara took the folded newspaper from under my plate and spun it around so Jerry could see it better.

"Aw, that's Lenny," she smiled a tired smile. Our bodies didn't forget the hour of day. Jerry must have thought we were all insane, due to the complete fucking uselessness of our answers to his question. I chuckled at this thought and explained.
"Lenny is some character that the county loves to use and he's based off of some legend out these ways. He's some 'guardian of the forest,' or whatever, but we just bastardized his god-status glory and draw him as an autistic elephant and sell merchandise with his picture on it."
"I think he's cute…" Sara said, as if I insulted her.
"Yeah," said Jerry. "He is. Just goofy looking."

An awkward round of giggling was shared amongst the group and I just focused in on the moment. The clinking of glasses and the pouring of fresh coffee floated around the extremities of the diner and the hush of voices filled the space. I was sitting with my back to the wall; Sara was on the inside of the booth, her powder blue hooded-sweatshirt gently shaking with her full-body laughter. Ted was smiling and looking at Sara, who was giggling at Jerry, who was wiping his face off with a dirty napkin.

There wasn't any music playing in the restaurant and most of our fellow patrons were senior citizens. You come to realize that the lower end of our generation doesn't seem to enjoy taking part in the waking world. I think Sara could feel the genuine joy that I was sharing with my friends, my family really. She rubbed my elbow and started talking to the others. I was also targeted in this conversation, but my paradise was broken. The hushed serenity of the quiet diner sucked towards the entrance / exit of the diner in a vortex. I felt a thousand voices screaming at me. I was in no immediate danger, but my heart began pounding and pouring adrenaline as if I were about to be stabbed in the gut. Images of the dead girl dying. Stabbed. Breasts. Blood. Knife. Dream. The horrible crescendo of sound and thought ceased. The glass door swung open and was held for a moment by an unseen customer.

The Swede walked in, thanked the person who held the door for him, and approached the hostess' podium. And he was all fucking smiles.

"We have to leave," I stood and reached for my wallet. The sudden jolt frightened my party. They exchanged nervous, confused glances and looked around, as if there were a fire that was hurrying my retreat. They saw no immediate danger. I believe Ted saw the object of my concern, but by then it was too late. The quickened vowels. The consonants where they shouldn't be. It was him. "Kevin!" I could feel his portly demeanor ambling towards me from behind. Please, please stab me when my back is exposed. Relieve me of this.
"Oh my word! How have you been?" the fat Swedish man pulled me in for a hug. Had he not realized that I was the one who punched him on our first encounter? As I was held against him, I locked eyes with Sara who was giving me a worried look, but, much to my dismay, this turned into a smile and she stood up and enthusiastically cried. What the fuck was going on here.

"Mitch!" Sara pulled herself out of the booth and greeted the other younger man the Swede was with. I broke away from the hug and forced a smile. Sara was introduced to the Swede by this Mitch and then Sara turned towards me. She waved her hand towards me and continued.

"Kevin, this is Mitch. We took classes together at DCCC (the community college) last year. He was a graphic artist," I shook his hand.

"Hey there, Kevin," he smiled. He had a jacket that was half a size too small and wore his black hair flipped in the front. I fucking hated him.

"Hi, Mitch," I smiled. I looked from the Swede to Mitch. "So, you two know each other?" I pointed to each of them.

"Of course," the Swede smiled. His ginger beard stretched with his animated face. "We're together."

Oh. Oh.

After about five minutes of small-talk bullshit, the Swede and his partner, Mitch, retreated to their corner on the far-side of the diner and broke away from our sphere of conversation. As they walked away from us, I realized that I had been clutching a fork in my right hand. Severely. Just seconds away from breaking skin, I released the utensil and it violently rang against the tabletop and fell to the floor. Jerry spent a few fruitless seconds reaching rather desperately under the table, attempting to retrieve the utensil. After failing and looking up to my eyes for confirmation, I waved him off, telling him, "Don't worry about it."

I sat down and Sara rubbed my shoulder, seeing my obviously perturbed nature. I smirked and nodded it away. It wasn't worth getting upset about (yes it was) so I wasn't going to create a scene. That fat fuck was gone and that's what mattered. We sat in silence for a few more moments, waiting for the waitress to bring the check and I finished arranging my fork and knife in a proper "finished" position. The knife and fork sat parallel to one another at three pm on my plate and I folded my hands in my lap. I just wanted to leave the diner.

"So, where is this thing, anyway?" Jerry spoke up, once again spinning the newspaper to his orientation.

"Fair grounds. Near the state park," I said, looking down at my folded hands. It was remarkable to notice the way my fingers perfectly complemented each other, fitting each other like an industrial ball and socket. Just perfect.

"Do you guys want to go for a ride after we finish up?" Sara noticed my stare, and addressed me, looking at my hands.

I weighed the suggestion and realized that I had no other obligation on this morning. A few years ago, hell, a few weeks ago, I would still be asleep, early into the reaches of that concrete determination of an afternoon hour. Alas, I find myself in this national-chain diner, the flesh under our eyes sagging and our general physical hue waning, and I realize that this actually sounds like a good idea. I believe Sara and I went last time, but for the life of me, I cannot conjure any visual from last year's county fair. It might be nice to see the grounds.

"Yes," I said, and stopping looking down at my folded hands. "Let's."

Behind me, through the dull and constant white-noise of the diner's conversation, I could hear the Swede laughing and his boy-toy Mitch twinkling his metal utensils. There's an innuendo somewhere in that.

"Yes, that's fine."

"And I remembered the camera," Sara smiled and padded her small backpack, stuffed into the booth seating.

Sara drove. Jerry sat in the front seat. His crown of suburban curls bounced with the slight whirring of the car's inner-workings and he looked out the passenger window, his head slightly tilted. I've said it before: he was terrible with even the most Platonic women in his life. Sara was the definitive example of that term, but she was also a bastard at heart. At multiple instances since we began the drive, I would notice her staring at me through the rear-view mirror, waiting to catch my eye. Having garnered my attention, and smiling out of the corner of her mouth, she would gently smirk, telling me, nonverbally, "watch this." One of Jerry's paws (for they were not crafted with enough finesse to warrant the word "hands") rested idly on the center console, as his daze dropped towards the coastal mountain shoreline. Sara quickly brushed a strand of her pale blond hair behind her ear and delicately dropped her hand towards Jerry's, "accidentally". It was like a fucking bee-sting. Jerry jumped and spat a yelp which was essentially the collective of consonants in the English language compacted into the span of a second. Ted and I, in the backseat, grinned like fools. Jerry was perpetually in middle-school in every way, second puberty and all.

The coastal highway was a beautiful drive. It was still early in the day and the morning fog hadn't quite lifted. However melancholy, I found the pale blue and dim gray palette fascinating, frequently distracting my tired attention from inside the moving vehicle. I did crave some rest. How much sleep did I actually achieve, last night? My spirit was high, but there was that constant warm buzz behind the corners of my eyes. I was somehow detached from this cozy scene, miles away mentally, looking in on this vertigo experience. A slight nausea was wedged in my stomach, its silver-dagger presence wrenching with every sweeping jolt of my stare, from window to window, to Jerry, to Sara, to Ted. Tug. Skewer. Pull. I closed my eyes and the discomfort slowly ebbed away, confirming that I needed to remedy my resting hours.

I woke up to the sound of car doors slamming. Sara was staring in front of the vehicle, bending towards me and peering into the vehicle. She motioned "come on" and Jerry and Ted were already walking away from her, talking. Ted was a little shorter than Jerry, and for a moment, I imagined that they were a couple. Jerry, the huggable-bear of the relationship, and Ted, the skeleton-accountant of the two, who would ask, spoonful of Fruity Pebbles halfheartedly discarded on the breakfast table, "When did we spend $500 at Circuit City last month?" and Jerry would shout, from upstairs, toothbrush still in mouth, "We bought my parents a new TV for their anniversary, remember?" and Ted would mutter ah and life would go on. But this was simply some voyeuristic fantasy that I had brought on by my lack of sleep. They were my friends. And I'm pretty sure they enjoyed the company of women, or, at least Jerry would once he mustered up enough courage to ask a girl to the metaphorical junior prom. I think of the girl behind the counter at the convenience store, the one who isn't Sara, and imagine that she will one day be Jerry's wife. This thought dissolves without an exact resolution.

I finally get out of the car and Sara is taking a picture of Jerry and Ted walking a few paces ahead of her. Undoubtedly, she is outlining their imaginary romantic life at home, as I was moments ago. It's still very comfortable outside, but a little chill, a little damp. I hug my sweater to myself and move a bit faster to catch up. Upon leaving the small parking lot, we are in an open field encompassed by tall trees, many of them pines.

Somewhere in the distance, an ocean breaks against smoothed rocks piled against a jagged cliff. Sara takes pictures of the occasional bit of wildlife and Ted is directing to Jerry where certain attractions and stands would inevitably be in a few weeks time, during the county fair. I am honestly not sure how either of them could be that interested in the subject. It was probably just Ted reacting way-too passionately about a subject merely because he was adequately learned in it, comparatively speaking. He grew up with it. He couldn't have avoided it.

The space was large and open. Upon wandering and following Sara's listless arcs, always in pursuit of another photograph, we stood relatively alone, hundreds of feet away from the two others. Since getting out of the vehicle, the small siren of a thought had been growing in the corner of my mind and it was now full pitch.

"So, how do you know Mitch?" I asked. She stood for a moment, looking away, through her camera.

"I told you, I knew him in school," she answered, not looking at me.

"He looked familiar. Like from the old days. Why haven't you ever mentioned him?"

"I don't know, Kevin. Why the fuck do you care?" she was growing irritated. I was being a prick.

"You seemed awfully cozy in the diner—"

"And this matters why? You never cared then. You thought you were so above us, the morons that were left behind to fester in community college."

"I never said that—"

"You didn't have to."

"Look," I was surprised. "I'm sorry. I didn't mean to accuse you of anything. I'm just… I just don't like the guy he was with."

At this point, Sara asked the Swede's given name with a question mark at the end, but I refuse to relay it here.

"Yes, him."

"What's wrong with him? He's a sweetheart. Have you tried his game?"

His game. Have I tried his game. Sara had bought myself and the two guys our own copies for various holidays and birthdays. Yes, I have tried the game, Sara. I'm closing the distance between Sara and myself and grabbing her camera. I'm yanking it by its neck-strap, Sara in tow, and dashing it against the ground. I'm running towards the tree-line, through it, and breaking it against the rocks. I'm strangling Sara with the camera's neck-strap, and she's dying. And I'm breaking it, breaking it, breaking it—

I'm standing in the field, looking at Sara.

"Yes, I've tried the game," I said. "It's overrated."

"You would say that," she said, dismissing my anger.

"But wait, how do you know him, too?" my stare shooting towards her, previously at the ground.

"Through Mitch. Mitch, from school. Like I said."

"Okay,"

"Yeah. Small world, huh?" Sara smiled. "But we all would have known him anyway. He's huge on the internet."

"The fat fuck's huge in person."

"Hey."

"Whatever, Sara. I don't know. It just surprised me. That's all. Mitch… just looks like a greasy kind of guy." I think of his slicked up hair.

"You just have to actually meet him, Kevin, and you wouldn't be so uptight."

"Maybe,"

"No, that's exactly it."

We'll see.

Jerry and Ted have procured a Frisbee, somehow. They're calling for us to play. Sara taps my shoulder and walks past me, rejoining our friends. I turn and follow her. I'm still thinking about Mitch and the Swede.

We'll see.

CHAPTER SIX

A beautiful storm came in that night. The group came back to my house after the park and we ended up watching terrible old horror movies into the evening. Sara suggested a B-movie drinking game. I suppose I won. Ted fell asleep in the recliner and Jerry was on the floor at my feet with a blanket over his head in front of the small sofa, sleeping at the feet of Sara and I, like a dog.

One big happy family.

Sara eventually fell asleep, too, occupying the space to my right. I sat there, unable to decide whether to move and disturb her (and possibly Jerry) and decided against it. A dull murmur of thunder would roll around the property every so often and my living room would be momentarily illuminated by a pulse of dull blue light in the seconds after. The rain was constant, but enjoyable. I absentmindedly found myself stroking Sara's hair, her head resting just right of my leg, and I stared down at her. She wore the expressionless line of comfortable sleep and breathed deeply. My fleece Star Wars blanket covered up to her chin and a small, plush brown bear character that was sewn into the blanket stared up at me with dull-dead eyes. Stupid creature. I smiled at the acknowledged distaste of the teddy bear in an orange hood and looked up. The TV sat idly, looping our last movies' title screen, waiting for one of us to click a button on the remote.

My hand still resting on Sara's head, I stared out the front bay-window and into my dark neighborhood. The occasional flash of lightning revealed the broken streetlamp across the street, and the woods to the immediate left of my window tossed in the storm. For just a single moment, I could swear that I notice a man in black directly under the unlit streetlamp. I look back at my TV screen, the horror movie waiting for me to click "play" and I snort. Fucking cliché. In my opposite hand, the one not stroking Sara's hair, I raise my almost-empty glass and continue my victory, alone. Isn't that the dream of every American male, every male who hasn't quite transcended into adulthood, but has long since seen the days of adolescence, to have his life become a horror story?

At that moment, Jerry, Ted, and Sara, aren't sleeping. They're victims of an axe-wielding maniac, they're reanimated corpses of my loved-ones that I've had to dispatch for a second time, they're vampires lying in wait, they're werewolves waiting for the next moon… but of course they aren't. A small smile forms in the corner of my mouth. I was never really a fan of horror movies, growing up. Grandma never really wanted to watch them, so, in turn, nor did I. We had other adventures, other vistas, to conquer. Nah, even before Sara became so irreplaceable in my years of acne and finesse-lacking motion, there was one other young lady who stole nights of thought, who ruined me.

Maybe it is just the contents of my drinking game expedition getting to me, or maybe I'm just emotionally unstable, but I begin to cry and think about this girl. Fuck you, Mariah. Fuck you. I feel my hands slowly form to fists, and I rest my glass on the arm of the sofa. I gently release Sara's hair, careful not to pull her into my irrational stupor. You had no right leaving me. Forget Sara, you and I would have gone on, forever, truly together and truly happy. But you had to go and fucking leave. Something large moves past the window.
Breath catches. Fuck this insobriety. Why don't you learn, Kevin? Why do you spend your days incubating your liver in a cool bath of metabolizing alcohol? Is your life really so terrible? No, you schmuck. It isn't. You're well-off financially, you have a beautiful blonde literally sleeping at your side, and two friends who love you, even though all you give them is an ass-backwards cynical shut-in critique of the world. I need to get up. I get my wallet off the counter and make to grab my keys, but reconsider. I don't know when my court dates and whatnot are, but I probably shouldn't be driving so soon. I'm probably not allowed. There are a lot of "probably" variables in my life. I'm going to walk to the pharmacy-combination-convenience store around the block.

My jacket ensures my warmth well-enough and the rain has steadied to a drizzle. May the gods kiss me with their staccato handfuls of saliva. One of the beauties of living in well-to-do America: a 24-hours drugstore within ten miles in any direction. Mine was literally a block away, just outside my neighborhood. Considering that I lived with the 55-and-older community, this made a lot of sense. The ever-expanding franchise of the 24/7 pharmacy logo smiled down upon and shone red in the mist of the dying storm. I grabbed one of those little shots of "energy supplement" that promises hours of alertness and increased performance (endurance, sexual, orchestral, I'd have no idea which) and I felt tired. Of course, it was late, so what need did I have of it now?

None, really. But the early buzzing of a forthcoming migraine was present and I wanted to preemptively blast it with caffeine and the like. I unscrewed the cap and downed the bottle as I moved my way to the back. It tasted like juice, battery acid, and cough syrup. It was alright. I turned down the aisle marked Pain / Cough and stopped in my tracks. Mary / Sally / Gerda / the woman from the post office was listlessly swaying, staring at the rows of painkillers, leaning on a cane. Aw.

"Mary," I could feel the tears well up in my eyes. I moved down the aisle and swept her into a hug. I never realized how much taller than her I actually was. As I pulled away, a long, stretching strand of spittle connected us, her mouth to my jacket's breast pocket.

"Aw," I looked down at this, before brushing it away. "Neat."

"How have things been?" I asked the wall. Her simply looking up and smiling, almost nodding, was all that I needed. "Great, great," I grinned, never once receiving a legitimate response.

"Well, listen, I'm just here to grab something. I'll see you around." I hugged the old woman once more and turned. At the end of the aisle, her distant gaze still on my person, I knelt and reached for my go-to brand of migraine / tension-headache relief… and grasped at air. The little slot was completely vacant.

Mother fucker.

I strode to the pharmacy's counter, demanding an explanation or asking politely if they had anymore (it was the latter.) I rang the old-timey silver bell that was placed near a telephone. Ding. Ding. Ding-ding-ding-ding—"How may I help you, sir?" The pharmacist appeared from behind one of the shelves of packaged prescriptions waiting to be picked up by one of my elderly neighbors. He was a few inches taller than me, wore thick rimmed glasses and a single silver stud earring. The black man in the lab coat was all shades of dark and white. Dark skin, white teeth, dark eyes, white coat, a glaring dark stare, silver earring.

"Um, hi," I screwed my eyes up. "Yes. I wanted to know if you had more of this." I shoved the PLEASE REFILL piece of cardboard towards him, almost leaning over the counter to hand it to him.
"Ah," he took the card and looked at me. "Let me see." He disappeared behind the shelves once more.

I didn't like the smile. I didn't like that he took the time to register what was said to him, and then unfurled this coy smile, always, before answering. He was young, but he spoke with too-old of a demeanor. He wasn't cynical; you could just tell that he weighed the value that he poured into every word. And I hated him for it.

"No, sir," he returned. "I'm sorry. But we're all out. We should be getting more tomorrow morning."
"Of course," I turned. "Thank you."
"I'll see you soon, sir," he nodded. What a fucking creep.

My headache ebbed. It was still there, the warm, distant, buzz that had continued to develop during my trip to the store. I hastily decided that instead of blasting the pain away with caffeine that I was going to drown my sorrows via an alternative route: sleep. I sidled past Mary once more and found a half-liter of night-time-use cough syrup. Ah, grape-flavored. I paid for the medicine (and my empty energy shot) and was drinking it like a soda before I left. The rain had subsided and the moon actually shone through the night. It was pleasant. The wind picked up every so often and stirred the quiet stillness. I kept to the sidewalk, finding comfort in the shadows between the bulbs of streetlamp light, and thought about nothing. It was a calming idea. But then I rounded the last curve before my street and saw a figure directly across the street from my house, in the flickering light of a failing lamp. I knew I had seen him out there before. I knew it.

"Hey!" I yelled angrily and downed some more of the cough syrup.
Perhaps it was the now-gusting wind that veiled my beckoning, but the figure did not move. Once again, "Hey!" He only turned towards me once I was within a few feet. He simply stood staring at my house, at my window, until finally asking, "Do you know what's happening in there?" I couldn't see his face. The lamp went out for good and the lingering blast of fresh light left me blind to his discretion.

"Excuse me?" I asked, pissed. He looked down at my feet, at my jacket, and then at me, and repeated his question, as if it was a common greeting.
"I live there," I said. "What do you want?" He kept looking at the house and just barely not at me. But then the moonlight caught his face, just right, from under his hood and I was angered further.
"Mitch?" I asked. "You're the guy from the diner. Sara's friend." It was as if a spell was broken. He looked directly at me.
"Oh," he stammered. "Yes, I'm so sorry. She, she—"
"She what? Why are you stalking out my house?"

"Your house?"

"Yes, moron, my house. Now go away before I call the cops," although he hadn't really done anything.

"Yes," he put out his hand. "Kevin, right? Listen, this is a big misunderstanding—"

"I'm not shaking your hand, Mitch. But I'm going to be a lot more benevolent if you go home now."

"I can explain," he was calm.

"Shut your fucking mouth. I am not doing this now,"

"Right. Fine. Listen, it'll make a lot more sense soon. Just a misunderstanding. Please remember that."

"Whatever, Mitch. I'll see you around."

Jerry was semi-conscious when I came back inside. He was watching an episode of the Golden Girls. I don't recall my television having ever been tuned to a channel that carries the Golden Girls, ever, since at least the time of my grandmother.

"You alright there, big guy?"

"Yeah, Kevin. Where'd you go?"

"The store," I shook my cough syrup, to show him.

"Oh," he nodded. "Thanks for letting us stay over."

"Of course," I said. I didn't recall exactly planning this. I didn't recall a lot of things.

I let them stay where they were. I made sure the doors and windows were locked. They all seemed comfortable enough and Jerry would pass out again soon. I bid him goodnight and he raised one of his paws in a lazy wave. I fell into bed and stared up at the ceiling. The bottle of cough syrup was still clutched in my hand and I felt the sticky residue slowly dripping from the tip. I put it on the end table and thought about Mitch, who was still probably somewhere outside. Now my house was being staked-out by questionable local gold-diggers. Questionable local homosexual gold-diggers who were involved with the Swede. I felt reasonably upset with Sara by this minor incident. Deptford County really does attract the best kind of people. Bring us your poor, your huddle masses, yearning to randomly stalk me. Fuck the people Sara knows.

CHAPTER SEVEN

I'm dreaming. I'm dreaming a dream induced by too much acetaminophen and decongestants, a dream that wants to break you up and numb you to hell. I'm thirteen years old again and looking out the front door of grandma's house, the summer after middle school.

The summer I spent at a sleep-away camp and became acquainted with my new classmates going into high school. It's the summer that I would meet Mariah. The camp bore some Native American name, but I couldn't recall it if I tried. I enjoyed playing with the others, but sports were only so entertaining. After getting tired and sweaty every day for the first week, I realized that I was no longer interested in such petty activities for such a pain-in-the-ass and lacking payoff, i.e., bruised knees and dirty clothes. This all really happened.

One day, we were playing a camp-wide game of capture the flag. Forty-some kids divided into two teams of about twenty. Our team's flag was at the far end of an open field and the enemy's flag was about a quarter mile in the other direction, across the field, a patch of woods, and just past the camp's dining hall. I was sitting at our flag, just within the boundaries of the game, and decided that I did not want to play this bullshit anymore. Sara was probably off making out and sucking face with some boy who found solace in scratching his scalp in the hot summer sun and sniffing his fingers immediately after. Deptford's finest, remember. I could hear some little snot yelling after me where are you going?! when I abandoned my post and wandered into the forest behind the flag. I shooed him away without looking back.

I couldn't have walked too far. Although the summer held nothing but humidity and visible heat for us campers, the forest proved to be noticeably cooler than the open field and provided adequate shade from the cancer-inducing sheen. The camp's largest lake was about a quarter mile to my left, through the forest, and I walked until I could hear running water. It must have been one of the many creek tributaries that ran to or from the water. I made my way to the water and sat down. This is what civilization does once it becomes too efficient. No, this is what rich people do when their survival rate becomes too solidified. When living in the suburbs or the penthouses of our cities proves to yield a minute chance of mortality, we go back to the outskirts of the developed world, just far enough away from a regional hospital or police man, disappointed by the lack of urban grizzly bears.

This was all a dream, but it happened before. I twirled a leaf in my fingers idly and stared out across the water, still protected by the shade. I burnt like kindling out here, in the American sun. How the fuck did my grandfather survive on the African continent? I thought of him and Billy suddenly, doing just what I was doing, except a million miles away, on the outskirts of some coarse jungle. Did they even have jungles where grandpa was stationed? This was my adult self criticizing the thought process of the teenaged boy in my dream.

"Ah, follow me," Billy excitedly smiles and waves grandpa on. "I have to show you something."

"What, Billy?" Grandpa didn't sound so amused.

"Just follow," he giggled as he slipped into dry greenery.

Billy and I (wearing my grandfather as an avatar in this vision inside a dream) meandered through the shrubbery, much like I had at the summer camp, until they reached an opening in the African woodland. "Billy..." my grandfather whispered. The clearing was huge, but still surrounded on all sides by trees that were taller than my grandfather had initially thought. In the center was a small natural platform of smooth stone and a large, jagged boulder at its midpoint Black ash and a coppery sheen were unevenly spread and painted all over the surfaces and leaked out into the dry grass surrounding the piece. I was slow to process exactly what I was looking at. All around the stone pillar and what actually appeared to be an altar were the haphazardly placed bodies of a dozen or so people. There were a few Western soldiers, a few native men and women, and even a few of the local children, obviously dead, in every direction.

Their wounds varied from person-to-person but their blood collectively soaked the entire scene, constituting the "coppery sheen" that grandpa had initially observed. Billy was no longer smiling, but appeared to be incredibly solemn, as if he knew exactly what they would find, and couldn't have explained it lest grandpa had seen it himself. "Is this...?" my grandfather began.
"Yes," Billy nodded.

Billy raised his arm and pointed to the large stone in the center of the clearing. Grandpa could make out the crude depiction of humans painted at the base of the rock and the large, poorly dimensioned being that served as their idol above them. At this point, I shook myself from the thought and found myself lakeside once more. Not six feet to my right, I jolted in my place when I noticed a small fox drinking from the still lake. He noticed my start and looked at me, almost amused. A red, sticky substance coated his snout and tarnished the white plume of fur under his chin. I was no threat, and he continued drinking. He looked up a few moments later and I almost expected him to say, "Hello, stranger," but instead, one of his ears perked up and I saw the thin muscles in his legs tense. He ducked and an arrow shot past him and stuck in the muddy bank of the lake. The sound of the salvo tore me from my relaxed state and I stood up, looking around for the attacker.

The fox darted into the forest. He was gone. I spun around in bewilderment and almost shouted "Who was that?" but stopped cold upon seeing a girl emerge from the woods a couple of feet behind me. Her incredibly fair skin glowed in the shade of the forest and her bright green eyes immediately halted my thought process. She had dark black hair that hung well-past her shoulders and held a crude bow that I recognized from camp activities. I don't think we were supposed to hunt with them.
"Hi," she smiled.
"Uh," I looked back to the place vacated by the fox.
"I'm Mariah," she put down the bow and reached out a dirty hand. I shook it.
"Kevin," I tried to smile. She was a few inches taller than me and absolutely stunning.
"Why... why did you shoot at that fox?" I asked.
She had been holding it in her off-hand from the beginning, but only then did I notice the disemboweled rabbit as she hefted it. She frowned an exaggerated frown and then giggled.
"I only thought it'd be fair." A retribution kill.
Mariah. I'm awake.

The sun's moments from breaking through the black and grey sprawling pylons of my state's forests when I open my eyes. The room's cast in a cool blue, giving no indication of warm, beating life. My world is subject to ebbing shadows and failing vision. The syrup coats my insides. Sara's asleep, facing me, unexpectedly in my bed. She must have woken up sometime in the night, unable to find comfort on my living room couch. I sighed mildly and turned to face her. She wore a slight smile, but held the displaced, drunk gaze of sleep comfortably in my face. I had loved Mariah; Sara was simply there.

CHAPTER EIGHT

Ted was gone when I finally pulled myself from bed. The work week had begun and Jerry was simply not up to the task. He called in sick and I assumed that Ted didn't want to miss anymore days. Somehow, Jerry was wearing a plain undershirt and a pair of my pajama pants. Even more surprising was the fact that they had fit him. He was sitting at the kitchen table and smiled when I walked in.

"I made coffee," I could tell that he had been waiting anxiously to tell me this.

"Thanks, Jer," I nodded. "Ted's at work?"

"Yes, sir," he confirmed my hypothesis. "Didn't want to screw his vacation time."

"Noted."

I turned to the countertop and lifted the glass pot of coffee that Jerry was so very proud of. I procured a small glass bottle and upgraded to Irish. I hefted the bottle towards Jerry and he weighed the option. After tilting his head for a few seconds, he smirked and nodded. He sipped and stared out the window and into my yard. The morning stood very young and that blue-hymn of the dawn's celestial waning still painted my property and the forest beyond. There wasn't a cloud in the sky and the sun was rising somewhere in the east, far away from my line of sight and the trees. I followed his gaze and joined him in the uneventful spectacle, noting nothing of worth and embracing the normality. At some point, he broke the moment and spoke.

"So who's that guy?" he sipped and nodded towards the refrigerator

I had taken Walt's obituary from the minimalist memorial at my former place of employment the day I had learned he died. I realized that I never really talked about Walter to my friends, outside of blindly referencing him in my blitz, weeks before. Even then did I barely go into detail. "He was one of my coworkers at the camera place," I said.

"Nice guy?" Jerry asked.

"Eh," I weighed the question. "Not really. But we got along really well. Didn't have to speak too much,"

"I gotcha," Jerry replied, his mouth struggling to form a visible opinion on the statement.

"Yeah," I said. "He's dead now."

"Sorry, man," Jerry tried.

"Fuck it," I said. "The old bastard probably drank himself to death. Ha, Mr. Hale."

"Who?" Sara asked, now in the doorway. God damn it. Having to explain something a thousand times…

I pointed to the newspaper clipping on the fridge and she immediately nodded once, understanding. I assumed she had read it before. She busied herself with the Jerry Coffee and picked herself up to sit on the counter. She wore a pair of my boxer shorts and an old band t-shirt. I knew that we could both sense Jerry's girl-anxiety, having Sara in little more than underwear, but we didn't take the normal route of action and tease him about it. The sun had been rising and the blue aura of my backyard had slowly begun dissolving away. Sara stared outside, just as Jerry and I had before, and started.

"Oh, Kevin. After your appointment, want to walk one of the trails?" she pointed to the woods.

I moaned a bitching moan. That was today.

"Sure," I exaggeratedly stamped my foot in place. "But I don't want to go the doctors."

I let the last syllable ring with a purposely annoying vibrato.

"Man up," Sara teased. "You need it."

"Fuck off,"

She eyed the diminishing bottle of whiskey and gave me a cocky look.

"Right," I answered myself.

"Do you need a ride?" Jerry asked. I looked at the clock.

"Sure. In about an hour."

"Don't worry, I got it," Sara chimed in.

Sara made me put on jeans and I eventually found myself in a hooded sweatshirt. She kept claiming that I needed to look presentable and I realized that this was, more-or-less, a court date as much as it was a doctor's appointment. It was a psych-evaluation, in actuality. The faded navy hoodie bore the symbol of my alma mater. Hopefully this could win me some points, somewhere. Perhaps a shirt and tie would have been better.

After sidestepping a bunch of walking white coats, I spoke with the young girl behind the counter. She wasn't very attractive. She seemed nervous, impersonal. I don't suppose I could blame her: she had to deal with schizos all day, working in this office. The patients were probably troublesome, as well. I sat across from an old lady (who reminded me of drooling Mary) and waited for my time to come.

"Kevin?" A nurse called from a now-opened door, reading from a clipboard.

"Yes?"

"Come this way. Dr. Mason is ready to see you."

"Splendid!"

I followed this nurse through the small, winding hallways that made up this medical office complex. You know, built to suit. I could faintly detect the smell of cigarettes on her person, trailing in her wake. I never really understood that: nurses and doctors who smoke. It made almost as much sense as the schmucks in college who would smoke and go tanning while maintaining a gym membership. I mean, why waste the time, cut out the damn middle man, eh? Either meet your maker or take care of yourself. Everyone's so afraid of committing to an extreme and instead kills themselves in the middle ground – a happy medium, a comfortable suicide. They'll take purgatory over hell. Some things can be black and white.

"We need you to fill out this questionnaire before we begin," the nurse hands me the clipboard.

"Excellent,"

"She'll be in shortly. Thanks for waiting," she smiled a shit-eating-grin and left the room.

I'm sitting in a small examination room. It's painted gray, rather, was never painted post-construction default, and the light gives out every few seconds. The window seems to be made out of plastic and is completely glazed over, smearing the solid outside world. Looking at the top of the paper, I see the name Agatha Mason. Blimey, she sounds like a crotchety old hag. Skimming over the questions, they all appear to be a load of nonsense. I decide to make a Christmas tree out of the multiple choice boxes on the right. Maybe they'll discover some Freudian code in the checkmarks. A motherfucking Christmas to remember. I'm giggling like an idiot at this thought and a voice enters the room.

"Hello, Kevin," the short, young doctor enters the room, extending a hand. "It's nice to see you again. . ."

I momentarily lose track of what she's saying and shake her hand. This woman has dark hair, dark eyes, and a bright smile. I can trace faint glimmers of dyed-red in her brunette hair and her glasses compete with her eyes in the catching of the light.

"So, we've been having a back-and-forth with the Deptford County Police…" she continues and I'm completely lost. I feel like I've had a thousand conversations before with this woman. She is incredibly accommodating and almost too personable.

"Excuse me, doctor," I interrupt her tirade. "Have we met before?"

Agatha Mason stops for a moment and glances at the clock above the door. She smiles and her glance drops towards her clipboard in her lap.

"Yes, Kevin," she says. "We graduated from Regional together. Remember?"

"Oh," I'm a bit shocked. "Of course."

She continues talking and I am running numbers. She must have finally completed medical schooling and training and whatnot within the past year or so. How very exciting. I was one of her firsts, presumably. Like Sara was mine and I was Mariah's. And what a fucking sham that was.

"Well, per the court order," she was finishing up. "We need to do this every week for the next couple of months." She looked at me with a look that suggested that this formality was awkward and a tad ill-fitting.

"But I think you're making absolute strides, Kevin," she winked. I couldn't believe it. I smiled.

"Thank you," I stood. She shook my hand.

She stood and opened the door to the hallway and I caught glimpses of her degrees posted on the wall, as decoration, as a proof of certification. Unlike the previous circumstances, even if I were to tell you the name of the schools, you would not recognize them. They were small and tucked away in the Appalachian East and I hardly could believe that they offered medical programs. Regardless, here Agatha Mason was, fully certified and assisting me in curtailing the legal system. She remembered me from high school and I had no idea who she was. Just before we were about to part ways, I remembered something I had read about the schools she had went to, an urban legend of sorts.

"Dr. Mason," I said. "I saw that you went to [
] – was it true, those stories about that nutcase from the nineties?"

She looked dumbfounded for a moment and then chuckled.

"Dr. Emerson? Hell if I know, Kevin. Doesn't mean he wasn't a legend on campus," she said.

"Right, well, thanks again," and that was the end of that.

Sara was reclining in the driver's seat, half-asleep, when I got out. I tapped on her window and gently startled her. I went around to the passenger's side.

"How'd things go?" she began.

"Do we know an Agatha Mason?" I ignored her.

"You don't remember her?" Sara seemed almost annoyed by this.

"No. Should I?"

"She was one of our closer friends from the group, Kevin,"

"The group?"

"The whole 'preservation society,' back in high school?"

I was drawing blank after blank.

"What the hell, Kev? You and I made the preservation society, well, the high school club, at least. And Mason was one of our friends in it." The silly little club manifested in my head, but the girl...

"I still do not recall an Agatha,"

"That's because she went by 'Missy' back in school,"

"Missy Mason? Really?" I smirked at the unfortunate alliteration. Perhaps it was intentional.

"Yes. We were in high school, don't hold it to her," she said, dryly.

"Oh, well, I guess she looked familiar."

"That's because you had the hots for her."

"You said that a lot, Sara," I sighed.

"You two just spent a lot of time together, even though you called me your vice-president."

"Eh," I tip-toed. "I'd still hit it."

"You're disgusting."

I weighed my potential rebuttals, thought of how many men Sara had choked on or sat on in the last year alone, but decided to simply snort once in what passed as a sarcastic laugh. This last bit of conversation had apparently not resonated well with Sara and I became a tad annoyed at the silence.

"Did you know where she went to school?" I asked her some trivia.

"Yes," and she guessed which university correctly.

"Did you hear about that guy years back, the guy with the gnomes?"

Sara looked at me and smirked for a moment, to see if I were simply fucking with her, and then let me continue. "Gnomes?"

"Yes, gnomes. I know, I know. Well, this guy, some professor, he was perpetually a few years beyond retirement, but loved that damned liberal arts department too much. He was a nut-job, naturally, but I guess that comes with the territory. Well, somehow, someone entrusts him the duty to maintain the grounds over the summer, something to do with budgetary pull-backs, and he ends up recruiting some freshman to help him out with the daily tasks. It was probably proposed as some bullshit 'summer internship' in order to get the kid to do slave-labor for next-to-no pay. Well, per the liberal-arts-dictator of a boss, he was also asked to keep a daily log of his summer job.

"The professor probably promised course credit as well, for the project. Anyway, he kept a companion log, in order to promote future iterations of the summer internship to happen, even if he were no longer in charge of the program. A teacher's guide of sorts, you know, what to expect, etc. Well, suffice it to say, the two are not.... healthy members of the college anymore. Both of them ended up as wards of the state, in need of serious medical attention and psychiatric evaluation. Two EMTs, a handful of maintenance workers, and an entire fraternity house of students wound up dead, and these two, the professor and the freshman, were found in a comatose state, just before the fall semester began. That's one hell of a summer internship, if I'd say so myself.

"Well, after all of this went down, they obviously could not ask the two witnesses what happened, so they sought guidance from their diaries. The first few days of the summer program were normal: the boy boarded in one of the empty fraternity houses for the term and the professor would check in on him every couple of days by having a lunch meeting at the dining hall. Basically, as the papers and the legend goes by the end of the summer, a clan of garden gnomes, yes, garden gnomes, who lived on the campus grounds worshiped them as gods and ended up slaying anyone who encroached their land. It was just unfortunate that their land, per their religion, was the formerly-vacant fraternity house that the young man was staying in. Ended up being a bit of a problem once the summer term ended and the new frat boys had to move in."

Sara continued driving and we sat in a silence for a few moments. She eventually looked at me, rolled her eyes, and laughed a literal "ba-ha-ha" laugh, a few tears breaking the threshold on each of her eyes, smearing some of her makeup, and blurring her vision. She slowed down and stopped the vehicle, to continue laughing at the ridiculousness of the incident.

"Are you fucking kidding me?"

"No, Sara. It really happened," I smiled.

CHAPTER NINE

"Can we talk?" I asked over the low hum of the radio.

"What's wrong?" Sara answered. She further lowered the volume.

"Can we... can we walk somewhere? The park? Just somewhere nice."

"Sure. You're not coming out, are you?"

"No, Sara. Stop projecting some sheltered fantasy onto me--" and then she punched me.

We went back to the park from the other day, the one where Jerry and Ted played out Olympic daydreams. I suppose being in or around Washington state implies that constant, that the weather shall be consistently comfortable, however damp and overcast. This constant held, as the sky was a soft white and you could swear that you felt the occasional raindrop, one that preceded a storm that would never quite manifest. She parked, I got out and stretched, and she then took a step towards the open field, letting her hand reach mindlessly back. I took it and we began our little hike. We moved slowly across the field, towards the thin, tall trees, and I realized how beautifully quiet the park actually was. In a few weeks' time, this very space would be occupied by screaming children, 4-H animals seeking a swift death in favor of another pair of petting hands, grills and wait-staff, carnival games, and the like. The good Mayor Fiorello was sure to be there, as well, absolutely dressed in accordance to whatever theme Deptford chose for this year's county fair.

The county staff always did a wonderful job of dressing up the fairgrounds and making it truly special for the kids. The Narnia theme was complete with false-snow made of soapy bits of foam and the iconic streetlamp; the Roaring Twenties was splendid, as well. It was just a tad unfortunate, however, when the good mayor would put so much work into a theme's costume (since he was the de facto emcee), just to utterly fail. I'll never forget when the theme was Oz, and the man dressed as your typical cartoon-criminal, with ankle-chains and an orange jumpsuit.

"Is everything alright, Kevin?" Sara asked.

"Oh," I had almost forgotten why we were here. "Yes, pretty much. Well, I just told you about Dr. Mason,"

"Our old friend, yes,"

"Yes. Well, it's about that. I feel like… I feel like we are always running into people and I just – I just have no idea who they are half of the time."

"Well, you're bad with faces. Not a big deal, Kev,"

"No, I know that. But this is different. They are people who we knew, who were big parts of our lives, and I completely blank out on them. You said… you said we made a club with her in high school?"

"Yes. A lot of our friends."

"And we were a nature society?"

"More or less. I mean, we raised money for a nature walk once a year. It was a field trip for a lot of the science classes. Otherwise, our meetings consisted of us shooting the shit in the band room, or you and I making out at your house."

"Yes," I closed my eyes. She was straying from the point. "I remember you—"

"Although, the doctors did say that this might happen after the accident,"

"No, I mean, I remember us, I remember our bullshit. Why don't I remember all of the others? I thought it was always just us."

"Well, maybe you fucked up your head more than you thought, schizo."

"Maybe. Probably," I looked towards the sky as we began entering the woods. "For instance, I did not even remember that schmuck, Mitch."

"Well, he did go to highschool with us," Sara said. "But I only became close to him after. But that's all in the past. I told you, Kevin, and you saw it – he's with your old friend—"

"That Swedish bastard is not my friend,"

"Whatever. You know what I mean. The last I knew of Mitch, he was dating some sixty-something year old dude. Salvatore, or something. He's moved on. He's not into me. Quit your bitching,"

"I don't care about that, I am not jealous. Like I said, I just don't like not knowing where or who all of these people are. Especially when I've apparently been in contact with them for years."

Sara was quiet for a few moments and then approached the question, carefully, anxiously.

"You've always remembered Jerry and Ted, right?"

"Of course,"

"Well, that's a start."

"It's something," I agreed.

We followed the walking path for a mile or so. We did not mind walking in relative silence, as it was a beautiful trail. The air, as I have mentioned, was infinitely damp, but it was not the humid velocity of August. It was a healthy body of existence. The green was artistically lush and the brown of the trees was near black in this oversaturated painting. Fog rolled in from every side, but never obscured our journey into the park system. I believe it was raining at this point, but the dense treetops sheltered us from the wet. We must have walked for a solid hour.

The thickness of the forest began melting away. We were coming out on the other side. I could hear the rolling of the sea, not too far away. The open field would break down into a much looser patch of woods and then into rocky shore. The trail we were following eventually evolved into a concrete sidewalk, now that we had managed to escape from the woods. We continued following it and Sara jogged away from my side and ran up to the informational panel posted. She stood under the wooden overhang and leaned in, squinting at the map behind the glass. Her finger followed a trail that I could not discern through the pale glare and I looked around, waiting for her report.

The path we were on ended in a small parking lot, much like the one Sara's car was currently waiting for us in, and the field was encompassed by the tall trees. It was almost perfectly identical to the way we came in, yet inverted. A bit of uncanny discomfort struck me, but Sara spoke and tore me from the stupor.

"Two miles," she smiled. "Well done!"

"Ha, I'd say," I scratched my neck and then stretched, leaning back, looking into the sky.

I felt various portions of my back crack and my ribs stress under the expanding pressure. It was delightful. I leaned to either side and opened my eyes. There, across the field, in a floral print dress (the one she wore the last night we spoke) was Mariah. But I know it was not her. Of course not. I blinked and she was gone, like I knew she would be. The draining ah that I had been emitting caught with my breath and Sara took notice.

"What happened?"
"Oh, nothing," I straightened out. "Thought I saw someone," which caused her to look around the park.
"Really?"
"Really,"
She wiped her face on her sleeve and looked towards where I had been staring.

"Listen... I know you have been thinking a lot about your past, Kevin. I know you've been thinking about your family, about Elsie, about the club--"
"How the fuck—" I was dumbfounded. She held up a hand. "I know. I know. You talk to them in your sleep. You've been acting weird and the entirety of today was spent reminiscing about kids we grew up with. I knew she was bound to come up sooner or later."
"Well, fuck me, right?"
"Stop. I know you're sick or whatever, but I want you to know that there was a time when you promised me that you'd never bring her up again." Her sudden fury made me smirk.

There comes a time in any relationship that emotional struggles will arise. Many couples, if they exist in an intimate capacity, will either resolve these skirmishes or let them fester. From there, the couple will grow and love each other even more, or let one of two things happen. One, one partner will take a proactive stance on the matter and change their habits (if they are the one at fault) or seek a remedy, such as couple's counseling. Option two, of course, is where the relationship will continue to flounder and ferment and die until they murder one another or part ways. We were at the non-existent option three. We were the fools too afraid to rid one another of the other's presence, yet so far and away from that happy couple you loathe and envy.

"Jealousy is an ugly emotion—"

"Stop. I'm not being difficult. Before you went and drove your car off Iron Bridge, we actually talked. You could occasionally communicate like a fucking human being. And you promised me that you would never bring her up in front of me. I didn't ask you to promise that. You did it yourself. I know you had your accident, I just want you to know that we swore that to each other." She was almost crying.

I could not discern any difference in my personality from before and after my "accident" – I believed this to be a fabrication of the emotionally unstable Sara's imagination. This outburst led me to second guess this afternoon's reconsideration of my youth. That is, I began to doubt all that Sara had said, about Dr. Mason, the nature society, and our friends. I took a deep breath.

"Alright, Sara," I said. "I'm sorry. I had not known."

"I know," she sighed. "It's fine." I extend my arm, in a crook. "Walk me back?"

She blinked at me and the hurt fury faded. She looked back towards the woods and moved towards me. She locked her arm in mine and we were off.

"We never did get to go to Germany," Sara said.

"Oh?"

We had turned the air conditioning off. It was unseasonably cool outside and there was no need to further chill the house. It was just the two of us, on the couch in the living room, blankets strewn about, watching some old beloved movies. If my house had a fireplace, I am sure that it would be lit, just for evenings like these. Her head was in my lap and I was absently twirling the hair behind her ear. Her voice had come suddenly, but still muted.

"Yeah. It was supposed to be our graduation adventure," she was, of course, talking about high school. Again.

"Yes, well, the best laid plans of mice and men, that whole bit," I nodded. "And, you pissed away any money you had saved senior year. I mean, we were ready to go,"

"Yes, you were almost ready to book it, too," she sat up. "And I know it's really childish. It is. But I'm actually glad that you didn't go without me,"

I sat for a few moments, weighing this confession.

"You are right, Sara,"

"Hm?"

"It is childish."

CHAPTER TEN

Of course, she wanted to spend the night. This meant asserting herself, consistently reminding me that she was, in fact, there in bed with me, but dramatically making it aware that she was "ignoring" me. You know, curled up, facing away, that song and dance. But I was preoccupied in my thoughts and her waiting game eventually gave way. She was too tired and I was too disinterested that she eventually fell asleep, her head on my chest, silently acknowledging her failed campaign. I remained staring at the ceiling, painfully aware that I was going to be dreaming tonight and painfully aware about the dream's contents.

The storm that failed to exist before in the day had come with the nightfall and its steady beat trickled over my house. I blinked once, knew it was time to face sleep and whatever it may hold, and closed my eyes.

I was almost instantly asleep and into a series of living memories. We were in the very house I lay now back in the land of the living, except everything was smaller and cheaper with the rescinding years defining our youth. My bed was not the king-sized that Sara and I were currently in, but a mere double. I felt a bit more tone in the integrity of the muscle on my arms and chest and did not feel the stubble of indifferent laziness upon my face. Sara was there, too. Just as she was in the waking world, on my chest. Her face was thinner, yet somehow healthier, and her eyes seemed wonderfully larger, more concerned, when she looked up. She was consoling me. I heard her murmur.

"Don't worry, Kevin. You did nothing wrong," she purred. "It's her loss."

"I don't care," I involuntarily replied, following the script of personal history.

Oh, I understand now: it was the last night I had spoken to Mariah. It was the night before she left my life and left me broken, in the arms of Sara. All parties involved were around eighteen years old. Oh, to be young and bloody stupid.

"We're all here for you, Kevin,"

"I know,"

"All of us," she assured. "Listen, we'll all meet up and go to the fair this weekend."

I told you that that was the only thing to look forward to in Deptford County.

"Sure," I stared at the ceiling.

"You've done so many great things, Kevin. You've brought us all so far."

I lost the meaning in her words. She remained quiet for a bit, stirring circles on my chest with her delicate, skeletal hands.

"Kevin," she looked up, waiting for me to acknowledge her. I obliged and looked down.

"Kevin, I love you," she said with the ghost of a question mark on the end of her statement.

"I..." and I blinked once. "I love you, too."

I see us, running through the woods, like a pack of wolves, along the trail we followed today, away from the fairgrounds, towards the parallel-universe of a park entrance. We break the clearing, I see the lesser forest to our far left and the entire field is bathed in a bold sheen of moonlight. Fireworks explode in the distance. I am still for a moment, pausing and taking this multi-tiered assault on my senses in wholly. The others, my friends, the members of the nature society, run past me, screaming, laughing, into the open field. I am stuck standing, staring at the moon, whose beautiful white body is scaled to obscene dream-proportions, almost touching the world, hearing the cannon-blasts a mile away, back in civilization. Sara suddenly, firmly, grabs my hand and curls up behind me, her chest pressed against my back. She whispers into my ear, her thin lips touching my ear, her voice, hot.
"Come on, Kevin. It's time."

It is the sensation of falling that wakes me. My very reaction rips Sara from her sleep as well. But, fortunately, she rolls over and waves away the disturbance with the ignorance of slumber. I can hear the TV on in the living room. Laughter. A murmur. Laughter. Commercial. Some schmuck won on the big game show or some moral lesson was neatly wrapped up in a sitcom. Either way, it's premiering to the no one that is my vacant living room. As I stood to turn the device off, I realized I was naked. My house was far too cold. I typically sleep in pajama bottoms. One glance is all it takes to confirm that Sara is naked, too, even though she is mostly concealed by the down-comforter. I sigh an audible sigh and scratch myself. At some point, we fucked, and I cannot even recall the act.

It is really cold in my house. The dull blue glow of the television paints an arctic landscape as I swiftly cross the living room, clutching myself, verbally cursing my own existence and the fucking piece of furniture I had just jammed my toe on. For some reason, I am still concealing myself. Oh, God damn it. I am standing in the center of light casted by the screen, equidistant to thermostat and switch. Do I blind myself by turning off the TV or fix the temperature and cease the relentless murder of my unborn children who are currently receding into my body? In a half-hearted, half-minded, I-should-be-sleeping stupor, I turned off the TV then moved to the opposite wall and felt blindly for the thermostat. Before I could even reach the damn thing, I heard the air conditioning unit on the side of my house suddenly swell in energy consumption. The vacuuming noise became audible through the walls and I was frozen in my tracks. I knew what was about to happen. And, there – it ran itself out. I could smell the static-smoke and the decay of the whirring metal, seconds after the fuse exploded.

I returned to my room, still in the dark, and toed the ground for a pair of underwear. Barely armoring myself, I stepped onto my front porch and slipped to the side of my house. The grass was wet with the dew of the dying night and I dropped obscenities into the echo of the sleeping neighborhood. I found the AC unit and heard a sickening sizzling sound. The smell that I had detected inside was twice as strong and burning my eyes. I could see that the grate that protected the top of the machine was threshed inward. Some stupid animal. Something. I could now smell burning fur. This was going to be hell to clean up in the morning. The erratic buzzing stopped. The unit was dead, as was whatever animal was embedded in its blades. The yard was silent and my feet were wet. I was still in my underwear. There was movement at the far end of my yard. I reacted and moved before I could properly think.
"HEY," I ran towards the tree line.

They were people, a few of them. Kids, fucking with my house. I was certainly not chasing them into the woods. Not in my boxers. I did not even have socks on. And there were pine needles and ticks and other things that I could not see easily with my unaided eyes that could eventually kill me, or jab me, and or make me bleed and fuck those kids and now I am going to have to pay for a new air conditioning unit and Sara's still in my fucking bed—
"I'm going to buy a gun," I cried. "And I'm going to blast the next poor fucker that steps foot onto my property."
I stopped and strained my hearing. Nothing. A few branches breaking in the distance. Then, one of them shouted, "See you later, Kevin!" and I could picture the inebriant laughing and giggling with his pack of handicapped friends. However momentarily furious this made me, it eventually made me consider the scenario and I felt a chill run down my spine. They knew my name and they were messing with my property. I do not particularly like Deptford County. I became aware of this fact at that moment.
"Kevin?" Sara was standing at the back door.
"Go back to bed. Some animal bit through the wiring. No big deal," I smiled through to her in the dark. She could taste the bullshit, but nodded and shrank back into my house, dragging the sliding door closed behind her. I was alone in my backyard, nearly naked, in the quiet of prenatal morning, threatening to purchase a weapon. This is not what I went to college for. This is not why I drove my car off a bridge. This is what Walt would have called me a schmuck for.

I wished he was here.

CHAPTER ELEVEN
"Kevin, there's nothing you can expect us to do," Ted scratched his neck.

Jerry was on all fours, reaching behind the air-conditioning unit, tugging at wires, moving dirt with his hands, and all-around being useless. I did appreciate his immediate hands-on call-to-arms mentality. I mean, combined, we were all pretty fucking useless, staring at this ravaged air conditioner.

"What is this stuff anyway?" Jerry asked from the ground, dabbing his fingers in the blackish slick on the side of the house and all over the unit. "It's like… it's as if a small animal said 'fuck it' and cannon-balled from your roof."

"I don't think that's what happened," I said, helping Jerry to his feet. "I really don't want to pay for this, especially if a bunch of those little fucks were responsible for it."

"Isn't your neighborhood supposed to have souped up security and all that?" Ted chimed in.

"Yes, they are," I said, acknowledging that I lived in a 55+ community. "Maybe this is what grandma meant by 'useless,' eh?"

The two of them nodded, staring absently at the mechanical mess in front of us. We continued the small talk and social commentary, we agreed that we should try cleaning off the purple and black hell that was smeared all over it, before the sun got too hot and started cooking it. I could not imagine what this could potentially smell like baked. Amidst further speculation, I unreeled the garden hose from the back of the house and turned it on. Capping half of the open hose with my thumb, I shot a stream of the cool water at the mess, slowly taking it away from the dulling off-white of my house.

"Whatever it was, it got fucked up," Ted said. Jerry smirked and nodded.

"Do you guys know anyone who can fix this kind of stuff?" I asked. "I'm almost positive it's out of warranty. My grandma bought it when she moved in and it was never a problem for her. Figures it takes a group of punks to break the streak."

"Google it?" Jerry offered.

"No shit. Just was curious, off hand."

"Well," Ted began, sounding somewhat hesitant. "I know someone. But you're not going to want him here."

"Who?"

"Take a guess,"
"The fucking Swede?"
"No. Who?"
I had no idea.

Sara had told me that Mitch had been in some sort of art program with her at the local college. I assume that his creative career was simply flourishing and that he did manual labor just to maintain his modesty. I am sure that was the case. Absolutely positive.

"A raccoon or something probably chewed through it," Mitch explained, further pulling apart the wire grating.

"Yeah?" I did not buy it. He says raccoon and I look at the air-conditioner and the torn hole is adequately sized for Jerry to be able to comfortably sit on the blades of the fan. "So how often do you run into linebacker raccoons?"

"I don't know, Kevin, I'm only working with what you gave me," and he turned back to the work.

"Nah," I said. "I appreciate it. I do. It's just... bizarre."

I then remembered the night I had found him staring at my house from across the street.

"Hey, we never really talked about that night I saw you out front," I started.

"Yeah," he rose. "I am sorry about that."

"Kind of fucking weird, man. What were you doing?"

"No, no, it does look bad, I know. But you have to realize, I was only there to visit Sara."

"Sara?"

"Yes. She called me one time to pick her up from work. That's where she directed me to leave her. I assumed it was her house."

"And you would just drop in?"

"Well, I never have before. But she did it all the time at my place. So I only assumed."

"Oh."

"What?"

"I just find it interesting how some people can become so addicted to lying. They can become so infatuated with creating these falsehoods and perpetuating their mistruths that their entire life is a balancing act, always keeping their plates spinning and the balls in the air. I could not care enough for other people's problems to constantly worry about keeping such lies consistent. It seems so utterly exhausting."

There was a moment of silence.

"You two have a strained relationship, huh?" Mitch asked.
"Something like that," I agreed.
"To each his own, I suppose," he said, rising. "I can't comment. You never know what two people are like behind closed doors."
I nodded.
"Yeah. Hey, listen, I need to run to the hardware store, do you want to go?"
He was fixing my stuff. Even though we met on the least appealing of terms, of course I would help where I could. .
"Uh, yes. But, I can't drive. Suspended license and all that,"
"No problem. Let's go."

At some point, between discussing where I went to school, where I had worked, and how I knew Sara, we came upon the topic of the Swedish programmer who stole my job. Mitch really did an excellent job of trying to make me feel sympathetic toward the Swede's feelings, claiming that he was really, really torn up about the whole mess, and that he didn't understand that his employment would have terminated mine. I told Mitch that it was water under the bridge (but seriously, fuck him) and that all we could do was put it behind us (fat chance). I found it funny that we crossed the iron bridge as these words left my mouth. Our past was water under the bridge, covering my car and the life that it had carried. I don't think they removed the car yet. Maybe they did. Regardless, the vehicle would be completely ruined, with its engine saturated and whatnot. And although it fully discharged during the impact of the accident, I wondered for a moment, if that to-go cup was still in or around the cup holder.

I then asked how they had met. Especially with Sara's supposed past with Mitch, I would have never assumed that he was banging the Swede. But then again, Sara did say he played for either side. I don't judge. People are stupid enough without analyzing their intimate lives. I rapidly lost interest as he started his love story, something about Internet chat rooms, game developer conventions, comic stores, and the like. He kept applying what he was referencing to me, or at least trying to, in order to appeal to me in the conversation. I did not care much for the things he spoke of and I let my non-responses speak for themselves.

We got to the store and he seemed to know exactly where to go and we were in and out in no time. He gathered what appeared to be wire and other smaller fastenings in a plastic shopping basket and we were on the way. I, of course, took them to pay when the time came, but I swear he would have bought them on his own credit had I not intervened. A very kind, and to that extent, stupid, fellow. I found comfort in his company. An hour or so later, he was bent over the air conditioner on the side of my house, trying to piece together what he could. A few after that, he was almost done. The aesthetics of the piece were rudimentary at best, but the unit was yet again able to function, and my house was back in the 21st century.

"I have to admit, Mitch," I said. "I'm impressed."
"You'd be surprised what you pick up around here, working odd jobs, you know?"
"I wouldn't, actually," I confessed.
"Yeah, the art degrees don't really go for much in bumblefuck,"
"I could understand that," I nodded.
We looked at the air conditioner for a few moments.
"...And really, I'm sorry for all that stuff with Sara, and running into you that night."
"Don't worry. I just thought you were some creep."
All I can think of is the phrase "sloppy seconds" at the drop of her name.
"We do have enough of them around here, as it is," he laughed.
"True words."
"Yeah," he smiled and looked back towards his work.
"This is the part where small talk breaks down for me," I offered.
"No, I hear you," he chuckled. "Too many people talk too much without anything to say,"
"Like that Talking Heads song, you mean" I mused.
"You know it,"
"Qu'est que c'est -- so how much do I owe you?" I asked.
He rose.
"Eh."

Mitch scratched his head and stared down at the machine that still lay silent. He looked off towards the backyard and continued staring, now into the woods. He was one of those, never looking to profit from his neighbors, even if they were financially secure and looking for laymen. Him standing there, his hands dirtied from the various pieces of metal and black from the grease, silhouetted on the forest, I was brought back to my youth and the days at camp. Of course, after my picturesque meeting with my dearest Mariah, we were inseparable, never really straying into too many other cohesion-deficient social groups, but Mitch reminded me of those other friends from camp, the other boys my age.

It was probably just the creeping heat and scent of physical activity that flipped the switch, but the thought was there, nonetheless. I considered asking him exactly how far away did he grow up, perchance he actually being a fellow camper, those many years ago. But I decided against it.

"Money's not an issue. Just tell me," I said.
"Uh, no," he shook his head for a second, but then looked directly at me. "But I know what we can do. Listen, I have a family friend, who needs some computer work done. That's your thing, right?"
I did not know whether or not all of our small talk from before actually sunk in, or if he knew that because of Sara's inevitable slew of social bullshit, in this instance pertaining to me, had primed him with a unique armament to be in my presence and how I function. I thought about his offer. He did basically work for free. Plus, I was not incredibly busy as it was, having since lost all responsibility. It could not be that terrible. His grandfather or some other old, on-the-verge-of-death, relative probably has a bad habit of downloading identity-thieving smilies or enabling an utterly unnecessary toolbar.

"Yes. I can do that," I agreed.

CHAPTER TWELVE

"Hello, Kevin. Mitch told me to be expecting you," Sal said.

Salvatore was a thin older man. I held about a head of height on him. He opened the door, greeted me, and promptly floated back into his apartment. The man was wearing a navy blue peacoat with large, yellow felted buttons on the chest. A regular Captain Crunch. He wore these little glasses that seemed a bit too small for his face. As he turned from the door, before walking away, I noticed that they were rimmed in a faux ivory and featured a leopard print design around the lenses.

"Uh, yes," I said. "He told me you needed help with your computer?"

"Ah, that's right," he nodded. "You're the computer guy." Sal moved towards his kitchenette and sat at a small counter. He resumed drinking a cup of something and stared at me. He must have had multiple errand boys running around for him, fixing various pieces of bullshit that he had managed to break. He just looked at me, not really expecting I do anything, just like an old married man would look at his life: content, not particularly happy, but not expecting much action in any sense of the word. I could not help but feel that this awkward interaction was normal to him.

"So where do I?..." I motioned with my hands. He tilted his head to the side.

I followed his gaze across the room and muttered an audible, "oh" when something stuck out. I saw his computer set up near the wall in the corner, but also noticed something else. Among all of all the useless handfuls of memorabilia and Americana I saw in the lightly colored living room, even among the general mess that decorated the apartment, I had failed to notice an older woman (a peer to Sal) sitting on the giant sofa against the wall. She was half-smiling at me. No, she was half-smiling past me, at the wall, more accurately. Odin's beard: it was the woman from the post office.

"Oh, hello. I, I didn't see you," I said. I fumbled with my greeting and sort of waved to her. Like a jackass. She did not exactly react.

"Margaret, MARGARET -- this is Kevin. You've seen him before, yes?"

"Oh, yes, we have," I said. Wait. Did she talk to Sal about me?

"Yes, Margaret. Kevin's been here and helped you with your crafts, remember?"

"I. Wait," I said. "No I didn't. I, uh. How are you Margaret?"

I was in an apartment with two senile old people. What a way to spend the day. Margaret just upped the intensity of the half-smile as her way of saying, "Yes, I'm still breathing." I still was not exactly sure what I was doing here. Considering Ted and Jerry were at work and Sara was probably still passed out at home, these two constituted the upper portion of my five best friends -- you're a real winner, Kevin.

"You remember her don't you, Kevin?" Sal asked, sipping from his ceramic cup. "My sister in law?"

"Yes. I've seen her at the post office before,"

Sal held my look a few seconds beyond what was necessary. The stare broke as he blinked once and lowered his mug. Placing it on the counter, he swept away from the small kitchen area and across the living room towards me. He gestured once again towards the computer in the corner and beckoned me to follow him.

"You see," he said. "I was working on my scripts. Plays. Musicals. Dramas. Anything that holds my attention until completion."

"That's fun," I offered.

"No. It is art," he argued. "But something recently happened to my computer and deleted half of my projects."

His projects.

I wanted to like this man. He seemed reasonably friendly. I felt as if we were old friends, even though he was in his early fifties (or just incredibly healthy and in his sixties). But I could not place him. That was the norm in Deptford: if someone survived into their later years and was not a transplant from elsewhere, there was a solid chance that they held connections to your personal history. He was probably a friend of my grandparents who I met as a child. Maybe he was an old schoolteacher, or cafeteria assistant, maybe even someone involved with the church. Who knows? I wanted to like this man, but if that was to be the case, he'd have to stop calling the eleven-page text documents on his computer art.

"Do you think you could recover them?"

"Probably," I nodded.

There was a chance that he had just misplaced them. Or Sal probably fucked up and got a virus looking at dirty old man porn. Did they make dirty old man porn for homosexual dirty old men? Hopefully, that would be a terrible existence, to have to live without.. Considering this, I pray that he has alternate sleeping accommodations for his sister in law. At least a room away and not on that couch. Even though she is far from sentient and mentally here, there is just a level of respect you should maintain, I suppose. I mean, I could imagine Sal going to town, bare ass on the office chair, headphones in, bathed in the dull blue glow of the computer monitor, while Margaret sat blankly on the couch, doused in a similar veil of blue, from the television playing syndicated reruns of The Price is Right.

"Kevin, have a seat," Sal said. I stared down at the chair and slightly shook my head. The price is wrong.

"No thanks," I avoided physical contact with the chair. I did not want a staph infection. Or a love connection. "Well, is this it?" The desktop computer was no larger than a composition notebook and a few inches thick. It sat flat on the desk and the monitor rested on top. "I could take it home with me, if you want."

"Oh," Sal looked slightly disappointed. As if my mere presence would have fixed it. He had probably worked in an office at some point in his life. Typical demands. "Well, if you need to, sure," he said and shrugged.

"Yes. Let's shut it down and I'll just take the tower part of it, alright?

"You don't need all this other stuff?" he waved his hand towards the desk.

"Nah, I'll be fine. This garbage is my life, remember? I'm sure I'll have the necessary cables and whatnot back home."

"Suit yourself. Thank you, Kevin."

"Of course."

Jerry and Ted came over later that afternoon. Somehow, Friday had crept up on us (although I would not have known the difference) and we had not done anything major that week. They had each brought their gaming laptops and were set up in the living room. I had Sal's computer rigged up at my desk, but I was still in sight of my friends.

"FUCKING KILL HIM, TED." Jerry shouted.

"I can't-- wait," Ted said. "DO NOT ENGAGE!"

"Dude," I could hear Jerry drop his mouse. I presume Ted let him down and alas, poor Jerry has died.

"Ultimate wasn't up yet, sorry," Ted laughed. Their gaming jargon was delightful ambiance.

"Whatever, I'm up in sixty," Jerry got up and wandered into my area. "What are you working on, Kev?"

"Eh, nothing major. That guy Mitch fixed the air conditioner and would not accept money. So I'm helping fix his friend's computer instead."

"Friend?" Jerry's face lit up. "Do you think they have incriminating photos on their hard drive? How old is she? Check it. Now."

"Whoa," I said. "Easy killer. He's a guy, first of all. Like, sixty years old, too."

"Oh, gross. Don't look."

"As if you had to tell me."

I almost felt bad for telling Jerry that. It really killed him. Oh well. He was rummaging through the kitchen, looking to refill his drink. As Jerry swept the contents of the refrigerator and around the room, I realized that I had not talked to anyone from the hospital or the police for a few days. I do not know who was more at fault in this case. The informational pamphlets and papers still sat around the house and Jerry was constantly moving them around. Hell, if they did not want to fuck with me, so be it. I would not break my ass to further assist them.

I got rid of a few of Sal's unnecessary and bullshit programs. His desktop real estate was literally filled to capacity with unused, mostly broken shortcut icons and I had almost vomited the first time I saw this mess. My OCD wanted me to die right there. I removed the underhanded anti-virus program that the store he bought the computer from had probably installed and replaced it with one to my liking. Although it had a few hits during my initial scans, I did not really think that Sal's computer had any Biblical-tier malfunction afflicting it. I turned towards the main goal at hand.

I found his file folder named "Projects" within seconds. After all, there were a handful of copies of it on the desktop alone. I condensed them down, keeping the most recently updated ones in the prominent folder and jamming all the others into a "to be sorted / copies of copies" folder that would probably go untouched until Armageddon. Among his other files, he had small collections of to-do lists and photos.
I could not help myself.

There were pictures of him, Margaret, and a handful of other elderly friends and possibly relatives in the first I found. Just old folk out and about, at the diner, at the park, driving in a car. They seemed to be a consistent bunch and most of them were cheerful, smiling. Sal always was (smiling) in the photographs he was caught in, but he was not very photogenic. His small, ivory-speckled glasses always caught the flash horrendously and he smiled this creepy, small-mouthed, half smile. I was almost glad that I had met him in person before seeing such terrible captures of the man. As sarcastic and condescending as he was around Margaret at the house, I could see the care he had for the woman in the pictures. He was candidly helping her out of the car in the background of one of the shots, resting his hand on her back in another, and even sharing her in a hug between himself and another friend, posing.

One picture really caught my attention. It was recent, very recent, and at some sort of local event. It looked like it was in the auditorium of one of those rentable organizational halls, you know, like the Elk's or American Legion. Plenty of elderly, plenty of chairs. Sal was in the foreground, receiving some sort of award. I recognized Margaret, although she was turned away from the picture, looking towards Sal. The photographer was sitting in the audience a row or two back. Sal was smiling, shaking the hand of another old man, holding the ribbon and gold medal that was being presented. Behind both of them, a newspaper frontpage from decades ago was blown up and enlarged on an artists' easel. A young man, presumably a younger Sal, stood in the picture on the aged newspaper, shaking hands with the man I recognized as my grandfather.

CHAPTER THIRTEEN

I ended up copying most of his personal files to an external hard drive. Legal? Probably not. Ethical? I would not know. If nothing else, it could provide some inebriated bouts of laughter later.

At this point, Jerry was face down on the floor (we were not even really drinking, mind you, that was just where Jerry chose to fall) and Ted was nodding off, watching the television. The front door opens. Sara is standing there. It had been raining, apparently, very lightly, but enough so that Sara's shoulder-length blonde hair was partially stuck wet to her face. Beyond the rain, she looked like she had been crying. I realized that I had not seen her in what felt like a few days.

"Hi," I greeted her.

She moved through the doorway and dropped a weathered plastic grocery bag onto the table. I saw what looked like a short bottle of whiskey, a head of lettuce, an individual carton of ice cream, and a box of breakfast cereal. Underneath her black windbreaker, I saw the name tag from the convenience store pinned to one of the thin straps of her tank top. The rain had managed to make the exposed skin of her chest and neck glisten. The black coat sat large on her frame. It was not buttoned and functioned more fittingly as a cloak. A white embroidered patch of lettering on the breast read the year of our high school graduation. I realized it was my jacket from those days, from our environmental club. I did not comment on this piece of nostalgia.

"Hey, babe," she was monotone.

"Rough night?"

"Yeah."

"Nothing much happening here," I nodded towards the two sleeping in the living room.

Sleeping in the living room, slight oxymoron. I wanted to ask her what she had previously told Mitch about us, how she bitched to him, making me an enemy when we never even had been properly introduced. I wanted to hear her complaints, to air her grievances. I wanted to grab her by the shoulders, Sara thin and bony, and demand to know what the fuck she could have to say about me. Right now, I am picturing rising in a fit, the hard drive sliding off the table and exploding on the cold tile below our feet, springs and plastic fastenings shooting under the furniture, the insufferable whirr of its innards sputtering into a crescendo and finally failing. I can see her recoiling at my sudden confrontation, her grip accidentally tugging the grocery bag from its place on the kitchen table and then failing, the plastic sack following the hard drive in its descent to the floor. Broken glass, booze, and wet plastic matting to the tile. The indifferent animate smile of whichever bastard cartoon character was pasted on the now-soggy box of cereal, staring at us, quarreling lovers, from the floor, amidst booze, raindrops, and glass.

How dare you bitch about me.

I am your daily welfare check.

I let you live. I give you everything and expect nothing. You are like a cancer, without the alluring prospect of death.

But I sit there. Looking up at her. A smile even forms, slightly. She walks over, lays a delicate hand on my shoulder and leans over me. I feel her thin lips (which were a lot fuller in our youth) kiss my head and acknowledging this sends a chill through me, to my feet touching the cold tiles, bare. In her crossing of the room, I had minimized the pictures of Sal and my grandfather on my screen. I did not want to begin to explain who these men in the picture on my computer were, why I had them, and that I had been helping Mitch, indirectly.

We end up managing to find a restaurant that is still taking orders and we get shitty take-out. She moves to get changed after hanging up the phone. I stare after her, watching the door close in her wake, the mood content and tired, and briefly resume looking at the pictures of a younger Sal and this community event. Besides the one picture, I do not see who I believe is my grandfather in any other shot.. Then again, the sighting was only an enlarged newspaper headline. Oh well. Sara waves and runs back out to her car to pick up the food. They were still taking orders for pick-up, but no longer delivering. I ran another scan on the computer, ironing away viruses and useless files and this stirred an odd feeling. It was like riding a bike as a kid the first few days after the doctors took the cast off and you had been basically bed-ridden that summer with a broken shin. Fresh, new, yet terribly familiar. This was the satisfying sensation of completion, of a job well done. As if I was back in the saddle or something, troubleshooting for some receptionist floors and level of concrete away from my desk.

Before I knew it, Sara was back. The food was alright. Greasy and portable, exactly what we paid for. And of course, before I found that sweet unadulterated blink, I found myself in bed with Sara, her legs wrapped around my hips, her one arm tense and extended, clutching at far handfuls of sheets, the other indiscriminately scratching at my chest, my back, her sides, wherever. Her eyes were big, tired from a week of work unknown to me, and we finished, coiled around one another, dead. We lie there for a moment, her, feeling the warm exhaustion of love; me, wondering what was the name of the dead guy from Stand By Me and realizing that I had confused it with the one found in The Goonies.
Sara is breathing in deeply and I am thinking, "Chester Copperpot."

She falls asleep soon enough, her head on my chest, and I begin to wonder how different my post-coital musings would be had they been with someone I truly loved. What if my relationship with Mariah had survived our teenaged years? Would we still be together now, or would my alcoholism and overall wonderful personality turn her away? Would I even be an alcoholic if she was with me? I wonder where she is, what the scenery is like, if it is pleasant in the autumn, if it rains a lot. I promise myself that these thoughts are useless.

My body is still heaving and I am still a bit slick from our combined sweat. I remember the first and one of the only times my relationship with Mariah manifested itself as physical. It happened days before she left my life. Figures, eh? Maybe she was not satisfied, but she never even hinted at that. She "loved" it, "loved" us. The moans and guttural purrs that her teenaged body produced could not betray us either. We fucked and then she was gone: it was as simple as that. Again, that's when Sara took me in a grip and dragged me back into her loose circle of Deptford's finest. Fortunately, I found some solace of my own in the company of Jerry and Ted. But like many prominent figures in my life, they were more or less just there, not necessarily being. Just there.

I wake up and Sara's gone. Maybe to work. Maybe not. I go into the living room and the guys are gone. The room is mostly cleaned up and I look at my phone. Jerry sent me a text message thanking me for the night explaining that he and Ted had to go help his neighbor move a couch up a flight of stairs or some bullshit. A handful of singles is on the counter, as a penitence for the food and booze. I smirk at this offering and organize them cleanly, slipping them into my wallet, which was in a drawer near the entrance to the kitchen. They were good guys.

I see Sal's computer humming on the table quietly and shake the mouse to rouse it from its slumber. The scan returned only a few hits and I believed that it was relatively clean. The diagnostics read positive and I had managed to increase performance in the simple tasks I performed last night. I go to the kitchen and make a cup of coffee from one of those new single-cup machines. How wonderful life can be. Innovation does not come from expanding, but rather, dumbing it down. At least for the consumer. I decide to be multicultural and make it Irish. Some would call it a relapse, I call it breakfast.

Sitting at Sal's computer, I decide that my work is mostly done. He did not require any extensive work, just some cleaning up. I take my small drive that copied all of his writing and bring it to my own desk, to my own computer. I plug in the small piece and wait for my own station to blink awake. I am still groggy, but thinking about Sal makes me want to dip into all of his material. I find a handful of files all named or loosely titled "poetry" and similar, vague descriptions. The one I choose is a small text document and when I open it, I find that it is only a few lines long:

> *Driving on the interstate, grand and inferior have a choice. The titans must run alone, but the small metal creatures, they may choose to stay with their own, or alongside their giant brothers. I always smile, as I enter the modern marvel late at night, when the "cars only" ramp is closed, typically due to construction. Why must they build at four am? Are there any actual workers present? One more thought stirs a smile: do the trucks and their drivers sigh at the sudden company, or do they bask in the presence of lesser beings?*

Sal was an interesting fellow.

It was humorous that Sal became existentially considerate over Deptford's highways, but I assume that is what happens when you live here for multiple decades. You make the petty something wondrous, else you become a victim of the monotony. I know that I just woke up, but I can think of nothing else to do but fall back asleep. I force myself to get dressed, properly, and decide that I should go return Sal's belongings and tell him that things are squared away. Maybe I will ask him about the photographs. It is not fear or anxiety that grips me, but a level of relative apathy.

I have a chance to learn about my family, my past, something that was never overtly concrete to me, and instead the allure of a couch-induced coma sounds more inviting. Maybe it is not Sal, but I who has become that victim to monotony.

CHAPTER FOURTEEN
"Thank you so much," Sal smiled. "My dearest Kevin."
"It was nothing. Just a few minor things that I ironed out. Should be good as new."
"I pray that you didn't snoop around, eh?" Sal smiled and winked. "You didn't pry into my secrets and learn that I was a member of some bizarre cult?"

I looked at the man, thought of the pictures of him at the old people club and considered that in some ways, yes, he apparently was in a cult. I was about to deny such a suggestion when he slapped my shoulder and laughed.
"Ha! As if!" he released my arm and floated away from the open door, taking my cardboard box of computer equipment with him. He nonchalantly dropped it on the desk in the corner and walked towards the kitchenette. His roommate was nowhere to be seen, though the couch was sunk in towards her favorite spot.
"So, Kevin," Sal said, pouring a glass of something. He gestured with the pitcher and glass, offering me some. I declined and he continued, "Are you ready for the County Fair?"

I had not really been thinking about it. It was not particularly a highlight of my year, it was not something that I typically looked forward to. I could not actually recall highlights from previous years, now that I was thinking about it. I just remember people and colors.

"Uh, sure," I said. "I mean, I'll probably take Sara and the guys. I don't think Jerry has ever been to one. He was really getting a kick out of the Lenny logo."

"Lenny?" Sal said, lowering his glass.

"Yeah, Lenny," I said, motioning with my hands. "The little white elephant-manatee thing that they put on all the souvenirs."

"Oh, yes," Sal smirked and clapped himself on the forehead. "I had almost forgotten. You forget that I grew up with the historical emphasis on the Fair, not the… not the consumer focus."

"I'm sorry?"

"You see, Kevin," Sal said, approaching me from behind the counter. He was obviously very happy with this factoid of local history. "Lenny is what we all call the creature now, but there is an actual reason for it. The Native Americans in the region called him—" and I am not sure exactly how many syllables he omitted or added. "—Lenikawaloo-tahn, but, being affluent Americans who wanted an easy piece of brand recognition, Deptford County's planning committee, or tourism chamber, or whoever, nicknamed the creature 'Lenny,' hoping to make the deity a beloved character."

"…Deity?"

"Yes. Lenny (Lenika… Leni… Lenny. Get it?) was a symbol of the utmost respect for the tribes in the area. A multi-faceted god in an era where that was not so common. You would have deities for harvest, for sex, for war, and on and on, but Lenny was pretty well rounded. A lot of 'end-all, be-all' as far as they were concerned."

"…the manatee?"

"Sure," Sal smiled. "Call him what you will. But that's just how the artists depict him. You know better."

"An adorable god. Terrifying."

"Hm," Sal tilted his head and then returned to the counter.

"Well," I said, rubbing my arms. "If you need anything else, give me a call. I think I gave you my number."

"Thanks again, dear," Sal waved after me.

I had a terrible migraine. I sat in my home office, the house nearly dark except for the electric blue of my computer monitor and the television in the living room. The set was on mute: the lights were too harsh, but I could not function in the complete dark. I kept thinking about the fact that Sal had somehow been connected to my grandfather. Whether ever professionally or not, some organization that my relative had been in had awarded a younger Sal. Maybe I would call him later in the week, to see how things are going with the computer, maybe try to force him into talking about it, because I had no substance to fall on. I was the one snooping, after all.

All I remembered of my pop was that he was in the war and was mostly the breadwinner in the family afterwards. I do not remember what industry he was in, but he was successful. Not enough to warrant any corporate inheritance or "family business" -- no, I had to go to school and marry a computer. I do not know, I do not believe I would have really had fit in with the country club type, anyway. I would be wanting to tear out some old Gertrude's eyes before our dinner conversation was finished. As for my dear grandmother, well, she was now, of course, deceased. Just recently. I live in her house after all, her parting-gift from this realm of existence. Mom and dad would not be of much use now in tracking grandpa's lineage. They were inevitably traveling to some corner of the world, pissing away their retirement. I can't say I blame them.

I needed sleep, per the norm. I turned off the monitor and slumped onto the couch. Some woman was trying to sell me something on TV, but I did not need foot lotion so I turned my back to her and faced the couch. Everything is painted light blue, grey, and black in this world. Everything. Blink.

I am at the fairgrounds where we all went that one morning after breakfast. We are in an open field, the border made up of tall, thin pines. I hear the ocean breaking on a cliff somewhere, not too far in the distance. I smell the fresh Deptford air. This was one of my favorite parts of the park. Something's wrong though. The sky is mostly black, but not like the night sky. There are influences of metallic blues and purples running through the stars, some which seem to twinkle far too erratically; others far too in time. The trees gently sway in a breeze that I cannot feel on my skin and I notice a beacon of light in the center of the field. As if a lighthouse or spotlight was casting its beam, a pillar of light focused on something floating a few feet off the ground. As I approached it, I noticed that it was my old car, the one sitting at the bottom of the lake.

There's a mist around it within the light, and I feel inclined to touch it. There is mild rust damage around the handles and wheel-wells and it looks like the interior is flooded with water, as if it were an aquarium tank. Bubbles float aimlessly around inside and large chunks of lake algae, moss, and weed drape the exterior. Well, isn't that something. I move to touch the door handle and the light snaps out. The car is no longer suspended in the air and it falls the few feet to the ground. The moment it was supposed to hit the grass, I hear a loud splashing and instinctively shut my eyes, expecting pain, expecting the car to land on my feet, something. When I open them, I am sitting inside my beloved old car. The seats are dry and I am generally warm. The water that filled it moments ago is nowhere to be seen. Correction: it is all outside. I am in a submerged vehicle, once again.

I peer over the steering wheel, out into the dark water, and see bubbles float away from the hood of the car. In this dreamscape, my car is air-tight and I am like the fucking Beatles in their submarine. Still staring out into the depths, I reach down and find that, yes, indeed, my cup of soda is still there in its holder, unharmed. I raise it to my lips and sip. Nectar of the gods. I unconsciously return it to its place and feel a cold, cold touch on my hand.

"Hello, Kevin," a hushed voice begins.

It has been almost ten years. It has been almost ten years and prior to this moment, I would have given anything to have heard that voice again. But right now, I wish for nothing else but silence. I want the car to implode, the pressure of the water too great, and to crush us both instantly. To die. I would give anything at this very moment for the physics of this universe to remember its obligation and to kill us both. In the waking world, this is my dream. But in this dream, it feels like a nightmare. These are the feelings that constituted those night terrors that caused my grandmother to rush into my room, long past midnight, and console me. More severe than the caveman being stalked by a greater predator, I feel cornered by that subconscious, sub-primal fear. In the waking world, I regarded her as my long lost princess. But now, her touch is too cold and her skin is too sodden. The voice belongs to my darling Mariah.

CHAPTER FIFTEEN

My eyes are shut. I do not want to talk to her. I do not want to see her. I do not know what has happened to her. She is a zombie right now, I can feel it, and I do not want to see her in such a state. She gently wraps her cold, dead fingers around my wrist. This was not how we were supposed to reunite. She again speaks.
"Please, darling. Look at me?"

And she sounds exactly as I remember her. Sweet. Almost sorrowful.

I eventually open my eyes, looking down at our hands. She is paler, paler than when we knew each other, and almost blue. My skin was always fair, and so was hers, but my normal tone now outweighs her greatly. My eyes trace her thin fingers to her wrist and up her arm. She is wearing a simple white dress, with a light blue lace trimming various borders and stitches. She looks mostly dry, except for her hair, as if she just got out of the shower. Her long, black hair is stuck to her shoulders and her back, and she is slightly leaning away from her chair, facing me. Her big eyes are completely void of any bloodshot imperfections and are staring at me, black. Like my spot on the couch, the world is painted in shadows of blue and black. Here, her lovely brown eyes are as black as the depths.

Her lips are full, but seem slightly chapped, if only due to their newly found blue hues. I can detect the slightest shadings of veins, just under her jaw, around her eyes, and all over her arms, like a hypothermic patient, or cadaver, taken from the flood. One of her eyes twitch ever so slightly and she moves, shifting in her seat. I react, almost violently, but then realize that she was only adjusting herself. She takes back her hand, alarmed, almost hurt, and rubs her own wrist.

She smiles weakly. I try to speak.

"Hello..."

"Hi, baby," she says, tilting her head down ever-so slightly, turning her eyes up to me.

She has a dark blue ribbon in her hair, tied almost perfectly, except one loop of it is tied too loosely and its arm falls, longer than the other. Almost intertwined, a piece of seaweed-looking material is stuck in between the knot, hanging in her hair. I make no attempt to remove it.

"Why... why are you here?" I say.

"Why are you here?" she giggles.

"You-- we, we don't belong here."

"I don't know, Kevin. It's kind of nice." She sat back in her seat, closing her eyes and smiling.

"I want to wake up now."

"Don't we all, dearest?" she said, eyes still closed, almost relaxing.

"Why are you doing this to me?" I was arguing with a dream. "You left me!"

This woke her up.

"Kevin," she said. "Stop."

"No, this is bullshit. Let me out." I slammed the side of my fist against the window.

"Kevin, you're scaring me,"

"No, fuck this," I moved in my seat and started kicking against the windshield, with both of my feet. The rearview mirror snapped off and dropped to the floor of the car. I kept kicking.

"Kevin, I am supposed to tell you something!"

"Fuck you," I kept at it. I could hear popping along edges and spiderwebs were forming everywhere.

"No," Mariah was now crying. "Please listen."

I kicked once more and could feel it reverberate through the car. A low humming now existed in our scene. I sat up and looked at her. The glass still continued to crack in places. Her eyes were bigger and now tearing, big, ugly tears forming and dropping down her sullen cheeks.. She grabbed my wrist again and then pulled me in with her free hand. She kissed me deeply. Her tongue was warm, but too synthetically wet, too dead, and I could taste a formaldehyde-like chemical sting that was not pleasant to stomach. But this was what I had wanted. Even if in my dreamscape she was drowned and dead for reasons unknown to me, I would always be in love with her. I kissed her back. Both of my hands surrendered and held her head. My fingers ran through her drenched hair. I felt a void behind her left ear, cold and wet, and felt a pulse of maggots. I did not care. I held her and we kissed. Eventually, we gently separated and she looked up at me.

"What did you need to tell me?" I asked.

"Oh," she said. "Yes. You really, really cannot trust Salvatore."

Sal?

"Salvatore? But why? He's just a loony old guy."

"Kevin, just listen to me, he's going to try and--"

Apparently my kicking was a tier or two beyond amateur. The windshield shattered and we were instantly taken into a sensationless, sightless void. We were drowning, deep in a body of water somewhere between reality and an afterlife I was not sure existed. Her voice was distant.
"Kevin?"
I drifted through the darkness. Falling. No, rising up. I don't know. Drowning. Suffocating.
"Kevin?" her voice was different, fading.
I stopped moving. The nausea subsided. It was still dark. My eyes were closed. I was on the couch. I could feel the familiar material against my skin.
"Kevin?"
I blinked.

Sara stood over me, her hand on my shoulder, shaking me awake. It was morning. I blinked twice more and then shifted, sitting up on the couch. Sara sat next to me.
"I was working overnight. Thought I'd stop by," she said. I sat there, staring.
"Is everything alright?"
"Uh," I replied, dazed. "Yeah. Yeah, no. Everything's fine. Just weird dreams."

I looked around, stood, and flattened out my shirt. I had crumbs and powder from whatever I was eating the night before splashed in the crevices of my shirt. This untidiness reminded me of Jerry and the powder reminded me of my medication.
"How about we get the guys, get an early dinner later, and take a walk at the fairgrounds," Sara suggested. "They're just starting to set it up. Could be nice to see. They don't mind, it's a park, anyway."

"Sure," I blinked. I did not really want to return to the site of my dream, but how was I going to rationalize that? Besides, I am pretty confident that there would not be any levitating cars that would teleport me to the bottom of a lake upon touching their handles in this realm of existence. At least, I do not think so. That would be unfortunate.

It was a beautiful night. The sky was a fading blue, rimmed with pinks and oranges. Clouds dotted every here and there and it felt like a good night for a carnival, but the fair would not be open for another week, not that you would even know. Plenty of people were here just to walk around, as we were. We had decided to skip eating first and wanted to see the place before it got too dark. There were long streams of bulbous lights hanging off of the partitions already in place. Some carnival rides were set up, but none were turned on yet, obviously. The ferris wheel was not yet completely installed, most of it still in transit-mode.

Most of the activity focused around local carpenters and the shopkeepers assembling their booths, installing deep-fryers and any other cooking appliances or display shelves, or whatever other oddity they were hoping to do business around. As we doted around, I realized that this was a microcosm of who's-who in good old Deptford County. Inevitably, the mayor himself would be walking around, but many local icons of commerce were already here. There was a dentist talking to the landscaping contractor outside of a booth-in-construction, which was owned by one of the big Italian family restaurants in the area. No event security was on hand yet, so a few police officers walked around, smiled at children, talked to the adults, and essentially mingled. Like I said, this damn fair was bigger than Christmas to these poor schmucks.

Because I always fail to remember just how small the world actually is, I still felt a mild sting of surprise when I saw Mitch crossing the field towards us. When Sara turned towards him, I felt her grip tighten for a moment in my hand, but she quickly dropped it and moved towards him, extending her arms. She happily shouted his name and embraced him in a friendly hello. After releasing her, he turned towards me and the guys and I shook his hand. "How's it going there, Kevin?" he smiled.

"Good, good," I said. "This is Ted," they shook hands. "And Jerry."

Ted asked how things were going with him and the Swede. He laughed and told him that life was good. They talked about photographs that Ted saw at work. I guess he may have realized that I was in attendance. I am fully aware that my grudge with the Swedish programmer is childish and nonsensical. I know I shouldn't make my friends feel like they are not allowed to talk about certain people just because I am around. But I also do not care. I guess he may have saw the look on my face, half-smirk and half utter-rage. I raised my hands.

"No, no," I said. "Don't worry about it. It's all in the past." Although it really wasn't.

"So, what are you guys doing out here?" Mitch started.

"They were showing me around. We were just trying to get outside. Lovely night, yeah." Jerry said. After delivering his single piece of information, he shuffled in place, rubbing his elbow and then not quite making eye contact from that point forward.

We continued walking for a bit with our newly discovered acquaintances. There was, of course, nothing really to do at a half-built carnival so we eventually left. The group decided that we were not terribly hungry, so we opted for ice cream instead. When we got back to the grass-and-dirt parking lot that would be filled to capacity in a few lengths of calendar time, I looked back at the fairgrounds. The sun was just nearly dead, far beyond the trees and ocean-side cliffs to the west. One dying hand of purple and orange fingers shot across the otherwise navy night sky and was falling victim to the hidden horizon. I heard the noise of scattered crowds still browsing the grounds, the break of the surf far below, and the gentle vibration of a natural ambience.

All was calm.

CHAPTER SIXTEEN
"You were acting weird back there, Jerry," Ted says.

The car is quiet and the dim lights on the highway slowly paint the interior of the car and rapidly dissolve at timed intervals. A gentle rain is present, but that is the baseline precipitation of Deptford County. No further storms are called for the night. It is pleasant and the car had been silent for almost a half hour up until this break.
"I just…" Jerry's suddenly wide awake and flustered. "I don't know."
"Were you and Mitch make-out buddies or something, Jerr?" I teased.
"No, Kevin," he was blushing in the dark. "Dammit, no. I just… he. I just get nervous in front of pretty people."
The entire car is silent. Jerry is beside himself in embarrassment and the rest of us are wearing shit-eating grins and holding back the floodgate of hysterics.
"In front of… pretty people?" Ted asks.
"Y-yes," Jerry replies. We all lose our jimmies and began laughing. He is obviously uncomfortable at first, but then regains the camaraderie, realizing that this car is literally full of his best and closest friends.

"Wait," I say. "Does that mean I'm not pretty?"

"I've known you forever."

"What about me?" Sara pipes in. She reaches back and places a hand on Jerry's knee.

"Sara, stop," Jerry curls away.

We're all smiles.

A few miles more, we are at an ice cream stand. We are all sitting on the hood of Sara's car, except for Jerry, who is sitting on the concrete curb in front of the parlor. The building has windows opened directly to the sidewalk, so customers can just walk up and order without having to go inside. The city is a lot warmer than where we were near the shore and there is a decent turnout. A handful of teenagers stand stiff, surrounded by the families and flocks of misbehaved children, and a few elderly couples sit on the wooden benches dotting the walk.

Ted and Jerry are discussing something about some new video game and Sara is looking at her cell phone, sending text messages to some unknown friend. She looks content; the guys, spirited. I'm watching the girls work behind the counter, through the glass windows and walls of the establishment. They are all, maybe six of them, wearing neon green shirts, some hemmed tight around the back, with black visor caps, all bearing the company's emblem. They all look to be around either high school age, or early in their college years. The one girl, the one who took our order minutes ago, she's smiling. She's either great at putting up with people's petty bullshit, or lost the will to be miserable anymore.

She has a very mousy face with rounded cheeks that glisten with the mild acne and hormonal surplus of youth. Her brown eyes sparkle in the flickering florescent glow of the interior and she bats away the occasional mosquito that breaks the threshold of the window into the cool, air-conditioned workspace within. Her shoulder-length brown hair is pulled back and falls slightly back under the restraint of the visor. It's her break now. Another girl comes and takes her place. She is much taller than the brunette, but equally as stunning. Her eyes are huge and black, cataracted by a shocking burst of grey colouring. Her skin is dark, much darker than her co-worker and her smiles is not as rehearsed. She looks content, but she actually acknowledges, even if she does not mean to, that this is a menial job.

The girl before her, the mousy one, no, maybe squirrel is more suitable (it's all in the cheeks) she's back behind the partitioned wall, behind the cooling machines and vats of ice and dispensers, and I can see her leaning on the wall, just within their break room. I'm watching all of this from the hood of Sara's car. I can see straight through the closed glass door, the fury of food-service activity and the large door frame into their back area. She's leaning on the wall, staring down at a black cell phone cradled in her hand. She occasionally sips from a half-empty bottle of spring water and looks up to the clock that I cannot see, mounted on the wall. Cheeks, she frowns at whatever message she has received. Probably bad domestic news. I know her type. Cheeks, I can see it all: happily steady with a boy at Deptford County Regional and they have it all planned out. The same college, an apartment together, marriage, and fuck, even kids. She wants it all. But the guy, he doesn't know what the hell he's doing. He's saying yes because she goes down on him every so often. She's saying yes because she's in love. He expresses doubts and ruins Cheeks' night at work. They end up arguing and breaking up shortly before prom. The boy finds another poor excuse for a relationship and the girl experiences legitimate heartbreak.

As I see this, a couple crosses my line of vision with Cheeks. Thirty yards, if that, and glass and concrete are all that separate me and her, and even with all these little shits and old people running around, only this couple has successfully stolen my attention away from this girl. The boy, he is probably seventeen and wearing an old military jacket that is a size and a half too large. Faded patches and buttons dot the breast and shoulders. The girl he is with is around his age, too, but a few inches taller. She is a few inches taller and has an incredible length of black, flowing hair. The boy, of course, has no concern for me. He's walking proud, his chest slightly puffed out, a cocky, thin, almost-nonexistent smile on his face. The girl, she notices me, I don't know why, and she stares.
Oh, of course I know why.

Her big eyes stare into my soul and I am looking at my Mariah. Not the dead one, the one who haunts the marine life of my nightmares, but the girl I loved. She sees me notice, and her beautiful pale cheeks blush rapidly, toxic in the artificial fluorescent scene. She squeezes the arm of the boy and buries her face in his shoulder. They are almost beyond me, I am losing direct sight of their faces, walking. I drop my sherbert to the ground and stand. I begin to follow them.

Sara looks up from her phone and asks, Kevin? But I am following the couple. There are too many people, too many terrible children and waste-of-space teenagers. I knee into one's head by accident and his bitch mother raises her voice. I look past her and remain locked on Mariah. I am making progress, but they are disappearing down the city sidewalk. I get about halfway down the block and they are maybe twenty feet in front of me. I react.
"Mari!"

The couple stops. The boy cracks his neck and remains staring forward. Mariah, in a floral print dress, she holds tight to the boy and flattens the front of her clothes. No one makes a sound. We are alone on an entirely different plane of existence within the city. They begin to move again and head towards the corner. Wait!

Just as they round the corner, the boy leans forward a bit, previously veiled by the copy of Mariah and smirks at me. It is now me who stops dead in my tracks. The little fucker in the army jacket is me. High school me. Kevin. I blink twice. The world is still a vacuum of warped silence. They disappear around the corner, gone. I think to follow them—I am torn from the dreamlike sensation. A fire engine goes tearing past me on my left down the city street, its siren blaring at a decibel level beyond my comprehension. It turns the corner, as if following the couple and disappears down the road, its red and blue sirens splashing back into my line of vision, its noise still echoing away.

I follow the path and stand on the corner. There is no one in front of me, except a homeless man asleep in a doorway and the fire engine slowing towards the far end of the street. A townhouse's second floor is on fire and there is already another fire truck present. Sara approaches me from behind. She puts her arm on my shoulder and asks is everything alright—and then she, too, sees the house on fire at the end of the block. She must stand for a moment and empathize with me the plight of the family who just lost their home. I could not care less about them. I am still staring in the wake of those two ghosts of my former self.

CHAPTER SEVENTEEN
We drive home.

They are all talking about the fire. Jerry's freaking out about how many fire trucks drove past at the ice cream shop. Ted's playing detective, mulling about loose wires and arson, and Sara's guessing how many people were hurt in the blaze. Me, I'm leaning with my head on the window. Each passing streetlamp is just another reminder of the glow, of seeing the fire after following those two kids. Every staccato, flash of light within the car are glimpses of the two, flashes of the smug little bastard's face. Images of my face and my high school sweetheart.

The guys contemplate staying a bit, but without a single word from me, they can tell that I am tired. I appreciate their silent offers of carrying on into the night and hanging out, but no such get-together will manifest tonight. Sara, of course, is staying and although the last thing I need right now is a romantic placebo, I certainly do appreciate some sort of companionship, some sort of breathing comfort. I had printed out some of the old man Sal's manuscripts, his theatre pieces, I forget whatever pet name he had for them, and they were messily at my bedside, stacked upon stacks of my medical and criminal papers. The topmost piece, the Yellow King or some other, was leaning precariously towards falling, so I pick it up and tidy the stack before replacing it. I realize how unkempt the whole bedside affair is, so I begin sweeping away the dust, crumbs, and fine blue powder from the papers, and correct all of the stacks into a neat order. I would probably have begun reading his script had a slight headache not begun to creep into my mind, along with an overwhelming sense of fatigue and emotional drought. My career as a theatre critic would have to wait until another day. Sara curls next to me. She turns out the light, extending a delicate arm from beneath the covers. Sleep.

The beach is pleasant, comfortable, but not particularly beautiful. The sand dunes rise only about forty yards from the water and are covered in scattered weeds and oceanic vegetation. The sky is blue and cloudless, but the world is not the same as our own.

I am small. I can feel my height obviously hindered. I am not resting around my typical six-foot mark and I exist as a child once more. I am accompanied by a younger version of my mother and grandmother, versions I knew before I learned the concept of death, and we are lugging our belongings on a small beach cart towards a predetermined destination on the beach, capped by a pair of flamboyant umbrellas dug into the sand. My father sits under the umbrellas with another gentleman that I do not immediately recognize. Again, these are younger copies of my parents, the ones I recognize from before I lived with my grandmother. My parents are not traversing the globe, they are not squandering their savings on seeing the world, they are actually saving for their son to go to school, they are saving for his first car, they are planning for all of the et ceteras in the world.

My grandmother, a stronger and more confident woman in this realm, sets the cart down behind the umbrellas and begins to unpack some of the rudimentary items, such as the cooler and sunscreen. I sit in the shade next to my father, almost looking away from the other man. In this dreamscape, I find no comfort in striking conversation with him. I am truly a child once more, shy and afraid, but not quite hating the world. I stare out to the water and see that it is not its natural deep blue and intoxicating green. Instead, it is translucent green with highlights of purple and black. Its depths contain not secrets, but abominations. Instead of inviting sailors of generations past, this beast turns them all away. This body of water was never a treacherous maiden to be conquered and wooed, it was a blight on humanity to look away from with pity and disgust.

A hushed, rasping voice, still strong and somewhat arrogant, rises from underneath the next umbrella. He addresses my father and then says my name.
"Have I ever told you the story about my time in the mountains and the monster after the war?"
I know this man to be my grandfather, although he is not looking directly at me. Yet.

In a gift of unknown and uncertified logic, the dream world allows me to know that this is true, that he shares my blood. Young Kevin smiles, I smile, and I shake my head. I do not recall such a story, grandpa, tell it, tell it.

"Well, Kevin. We were in a small village during the fall. They had made sure that we had arrived just before the bad storms did. Terrible snow, chilling cold. In northern Europe, it was normally chilly, as it was, but those winters would kill you where you stood. The war was winding down, hell, it might even had been over by this point, but we were to spend the remaining autumn and winter there, just for peacekeeping purposes. At some point, this little village may have been a halfway point for the enemy supply route. I suppose we were just making sure things were kosher.

"Anyways, Billy was, by now, in our ranks as your typical recruit. The campaign in Africa was over and we all loved giving him a hard time about the weather. By far he was not used to it. Should have seen him flip when he first saw the snow. He was a good man. Funny, good storyteller, the European broads loved him, absolutely loved him... right. So, it was Billy and I and about a hundred or so others. We had occupied this old youth group or patrol barracks, I don't know. You know how those little nothing-countries were. They either had a militia or a patrol to keep the damn gypsies out, or for avalanche watches, all that stupid fairy-tale nonsense. Regardless, the war was over, their largest building with plenty of bunks was empty, and they were having the Americans and their friends over for a giant slumber party.

"We got along with the locals. Most were quiet, but welcoming, people. Most were just trying to stay alive in the middle-of-nowhere mountain town. It was a pretty comfortable lifestyle. A lot of them worked in the valley during the warmer seasons, but the ground was pure ice when we were there. The guys I was with, we'd have to divvy the patrol jobs up between a hundred men, so most of our time was spent at the bar or trying our hand at flirtation in broken languages with the broken girls. They loved our English, though the Lord only knows that they had no idea what we were ever saying. And again, they loved Billy. Christ, his African nonsense and their unintelligible hushes of phrases and coyness, it was just a comfortable place to be.

And then a child went missing.

"We were sitting in the main room of a tavern in the square. It was just before sundown, but the entire mountainside and village was veiled in the light blue and pink of a dying day. Light snow was beginning to fall, and Billy was going toe-to-toe with one of our British buddies in a drinking contest. Billy had this young blonde next to him, holding onto his arm and cheering. The British guy, he had his shrieking fanbase within arms reach. Other men were scattered about the bar with their respective cliques and a few locals were there, just passing the time. Our group was still merrily drunk and obnoxiously loud, when I realized that we were soon the only ones at such a decibel level. I looked around as the other tables' conversations simmered and cleared my throat in the direction of my friends. The girls stop laughing and look past me. I turn and I see this old decrepit woman approaching the center of the room, close to our table.

"'You monsters,' she says. She's waving a bony hand at all of us. 'You let the beasts from beyond the gates take our children. You let these wild animals run rampant. We were perfectly fine before your lot came in.'

"Of course, this is all in broken slurs in almost-English. Some of my friends give me 'get a load of this' glances, but we're all listening to her. We ask what she meant, if anything happened, and we learn that one of her granddaughter's friends is missing and her family is beside themselves. We don't know what to do. One of the locals goes to consoles her, murmurs something to the bartender, and the barman politely suggests that we all go home for the night. We were a little ticked, but we realized that this woman's grieving was a bit more important than our drinking.

"So we send a few more men on patrol each night that week and we send them a little bit further outside of the perimeter than normal. About a week goes by and nothing shows up. Then, Saturday night, one of the groups finds and shoots down a large bear that was found prowling around near where the town dumps most of their garbage. The thing was covered in blood, literally covered, and since it was feeling very wintery out, no one believed that the bear's hunting habits could be so adequately quenched on the scarce wildlife. We all assumed that he must have attacked the little girl. The girl's family agreed. And although it fucking tore at them to know their little girl was dead, at least they had closure.

"Well, that's until a week later and another little shit gets taken away. The locals are beyond upset with us. 'You brought this evil,' or 'your equipment must be luring these beasts,' and some even got religious saying that we were attracting demons, and all that. We felt bad, yes, but what could we do? All the higher-ups could do was put more bodies on patrol and cut into our relaxation time. It was annoying, but at least it gave us something to do. We couldn't find any more animals on patrol, so we assumed this kid wandered off. I mean, I know many of us wanted to at times. Such a bleak, gray village. The only sunlight shone through sheets of white during the day.

"We become complacent, dulled to this inactivity. Two more children disappear. People start getting paranoid. Many of the villagers don't trust us. The bartender, sort of a local mayor, he still likes us, and starts warning us to stay in the square or our barracks. Don't wander at night, we don't know how an upset family could retaliate. The big guys start talking about leaving the town early, before spring, even though the winter roads are more or less suicide. But we're not wanted here anymore.

"This is driven home when one of our own guys disappears. And another one, named Peters. This is no longer a boogeyman stealing little European children. This was a mild act of war. All men are now are now on high alert. I'll never forget, I was leaning against the wall of one of the town's gates, the main thoroughfare into the place, staring out onto the road, cutting into the forest and then, the mountains. For the first time since winter fell, we heard noises from the outside. Howling, lots of it. No one had acted yet.

"The next evening, after more hourly howling, they decide to send a group of men out to investigate. They walk a mile or two onto the road and then follow the noises off the path and into the woods. In the shadow of a mountain, they find an opening to a cave, a cave with dancing shadows and patterns of activity painting its walls from inside. They go into the cave and see that the light is coming from deep, deep within. They hear a single man shouting in a grisly rage and the pained howling and whining of wolves. They shout in the local tongue, 'we are friendly military men, do you need assistance?' and the howling and speaking stops.

"The light at the end flickers and goes out. They are faced with silence. The men turn on their lanterns and proceed, warning in the local language that they are armed and are looking for missing people. They get to the end of the cave, well, at least what appears to be the end – it ends up splintering off into a hundred different smaller tunnels, but that's beside the point – and they find the missing people. Peters, he's there, still mostly in his uniform, but his eyes are gouged out and his tongue is missing. He's dead. They find the children, a bit cleaner of kills, and they are laid around the bottom of this stone altar. A still-breathing wolf is laid across the top, but its back is terribly broken and the damn thing is sitting there whimpering. One of the men walks up and fires once into its head, putting it out of its misery.

"Well, as soon as he fires and the occupants of the cave are momentarily deafened due to the echoing blast, a man comes screaming from the extremities of the room, shirtless and covered in blood. He's holding a large, rusty scimitar, from either the African continent or somewhere in the Far East. There is no reasoning with him, the men raise their guns and fire at his midsection. A few shots miss, given that they are in the dark of a cave, but one pierces his chest, just near his heart, but closer to center.

"Turns out, one of their own went stir crazy up there. Discovered something dark. Began practicing this occult bullshit, or was just hiding in a cave, eating people. They didn't know. They never investigated exactly what he was trying to do. The unit brought the bodies back and I remember the looks on their faces, the citizens. They were terrified, but knew that it was not the military's doing – just one of them gone crazy, missing the sun, missing the pregnant world. That did not rid them of their spite, hell no. They still hated us. We were gone in a couple of weeks anyway. They had their funerals for the children and the unit had a small memorial for Peters before his body was sent home."

My grandpa took a small glass vial out of his pocket, uncorked it, and drew a small line of powder on his wrist. He briskly sniffs the substance and it is gone. He grimaces, smirks, and continues looking at the dark ocean. He holds the small bottle out to my father and he declines. He turns towards me, six year old me, and begins to offer, when my father cuts him off, his voice breaking at first," D-don't you dare, pop," he said. He finished the sentence with a nervous giggle.

"Fine," grandpa says. "It typically skips a generation, anyway."
I sit there for a few moments and stir my feet in the sand of the beach. The little crystals of glass that we are so familiar with, the little clear pieces of mineral that we all know in our world, are replaced by little purple and blue bits of what I can only refer to as diamonds. It is normal in this realm. I look up, towards the water and then towards my grandfather.

"Grandpa," I ask. "Why did that soldier kill a wolf?"

Grandpa stands there for a moment, recaps the vial and drops it into his pocket. He picks me up and turns to face the women of my family near the umbrella. He has ignored my question and tells my grandmother to take a photograph of us with her camera. It is one of those old-fashioned ones, severely old-fashioned. She rigs the device up onto a small wooden stool and veils herself underneath the blackout curtain. She raises her baton and the large, obnoxious bulb remains unbroken, having no need for a flash on this beach. With me still in his arms, he turns us towards the water. He walks towards the dark mess and with it licking at his feet, stops, just staring out, enjoying it.

"What do we do when the abyss calls, Kevin?"

We stand there for what feels like hours. I struggle to turn back to my family, but they are gone. Most of the beach is, as well. Feet behind us, a dark, tangled forest has replaced most of the bizarre, sandy beach. The sky is darker, as is the world. I do not formulate a response. He, instead, responds to his own question.

"We answer."

CHAPTER EIGHTEEN
"Was your grandpa always the crazy prophet fisherman from Jaws?"
There was a reason I did not open up to my friends.

"No, Ted. I don't even know him. He died a long time ago. A few years after I was born, I think. He was never in the picture. He gave our family military health benefits and a handful of good stories and antiques. Mom and dad refuse to talk about him and grandma's dead. But I do remember him, very, very loosely."
"Oh," Ted says. "I'm sorry."
"It's nothing. Don't worry."
"You know we're just concerned, dude. We just don't want to see another… incident happen, you know?"
I think of my car at the bottom of the lake.
"Yes, I know."
Jerry was scraping at the bottom of his ceramic bowl with his fork. He had ordered oatmeal and was simply not content to move onto the latter portion of his breakfast. The waitress watched, amused, from behind the diner's bar section. Some people get dogs to attract the opposite sex. They had an adorable being of a lesser intelligence around to make small talk about and watch in joyful stupidity. We had Jerry.

Jerry and Ted begin talking about something that was going on at work and I place Sal's manuscript on the table. The Yellowed King. I can see that this is some play on a weird fiction classic. I cannot remember the original's name and I would not be bothered to lie about having read it, but I know it exists. The first page after the title is a list of characters. There are a handful of names with far too many vowels and syllables and I roll my eyes at Sal's character creation. But the three main characters are named Virgil, the Poet, and the Lover. Everyone else is a bastardization of some Roman-sounding name, or a type of salad dressing.

The world he paints is beautiful, I must admit. Rolling hills of golden wheat and golden vegetation, and things beyond our normalcy. Forests full of sparkling wood and twilighted charm. Purple skies and shrubbery that does not pierce the flesh. Wonder, beauty. Sal is obviously the narrator of the character Virgil. He is all knowing, all telling, and all fabulous. He knows everything there is to know about the Poet and his Lover. The Lover is a blundering fool, star-crossed and confused. The Poet is relatively knowing and callous. The Lover is not keen to the Poet's underhanded doings. Jerry sneezes loudly and snot-rockets onto the table.

"Ahhhhhhh…" he whines and clutches a hand to his nose, rising and exiting the table and retreating to the bathroom.

Apparently, he was not as stupid as we had believed and may have actually known that the waitress was eying him up. He knew he was under the microscope and he fucking blew it.

I am half-reading and half-seeing how quickly I can get through these pages. It is formatted properly and is not difficult, but you know I was never really one for theatre. A page I am passing over catches my eye and I turn back. There on top is a simple statement: THE FAMILY BUSINESS AND THE ROYAL BLOOD. Oh, Salvatore. I wonder if he is a stoner. He is a bit more finessed and better-dressing than the old hippies I know of in the area, but I know far too many almost-millionaires who partake in the same pastime. The Poet is holding his Lover in his arms and is crying, sobbing into open wounds and blood. From an omnipotent distance, Virgil is bowing his head and writing on a length of parchment, stating his sympathies for the two, poor bastards, writing concurrently to the tragic scene, accounting for it in its entirety.

His thoughts ebb through the narrative as the Lover's blood seeps through the Poet's fingers. Virgil is miles away, in a tower half-submerged in a swamp. He describes himself as wearing sodden clothes and his skin is damp with decay. The pale glow of his only remaining candle is dying.

He knows this because Sal knows this, he writes this because Sal wrote it. Virgil gives a hint of helplessness, the curse of knowing all but being contained within a mortal body that is truly incapable of being a savior. Not only that, but he is far too away from the actual scene. He is a mystic, after all, visible of sight, yet incapable of action. I cannot discern the actual tragedy at hand, I had only skimmed the play up until this point. The Poet slowly lowers the body of his Lover and stands. I expect him, per Sal's dramatic tendencies, to shout towards the heavens, to curse whoever did this, but instead, he looks down and sighs. Even through the text of an aging hipster old man, I can feel the gravity of this scene and the emotions it carries. The Poet's lips flatten into an almost smile and he holds out his hands to be cleansed in this newly manifested rain, as they are outside. He sits down, dead leaves and dirt all around him, and sits in a meditative pose. Blaring creatures begin to surround him from far away. They are rapidly descending upon his location. He sits, his palms towards the sky, content in the rain, and simply says, "I am ready to go."

The act ends at the closure of this scene. There are only a few pages left of the play, so I wonder exactly what this means, where is he going, who are the creatures that are closing on him – then the waitress drops a handful of silverware two tables down and bends over to retrieve them. This is as much of a sight that I need to be distracted from an old man's writing.

Jerry comes back to the table, embarrassed, his nose red from the friction of cleaning himself, and connects the dots of my eyes to this waitress' backside.

"You're a pig," he sits down, as if I hurt his honor. As if they were destined to get married, have a dozen hideous children, and to retire in Deptford.

"She dropped the forks," I offer.

"And the sky is blue. And you are a pig," Jerry deadpans.

"Will there be anything else this morning?" the waitress popped up.

Ted and I shook our heads and reached for our wallets. My eyes shot towards the waitress' nametag and I read "Mildred" – I mentally dry heaved at the name, but any social nausea was about to be blown away by what our Jerry did.

"Oh, no thanks, Millie," Jerry said, without a stutter. Without a hint of anxiety. Without staring at her chest the entire time. He made a pet name out of nametag. "Everything was wonderful."

By the vengeful gods, by Carl Sagan and every driven scientist, by every kid who ever took apart the remote control just to see how his world worked, by the very nature of the universe alone, I was astounded. As she left to retrieve the bill, Ted and I stared, dumbfounded at our boy.

"What?" Jerry asked, obviously proud. "She helped me out when I had my accident (referring to his hasty retreat to the bathroom that we had not paid enough attention to). You two dinks were too evil hearted to bother to help me."

Ted clapped him on the shoulder. We paid the tab and left. There was a phone number on the receipt for Jerry.

CHAPTER NINETEEN

I was in a good mood. As often as I like to badmouth my friends' social failings, it was a nice change of pace to experience one of them growing. Jerry, more so than Ted.

Ted was a lot more on-base and stable than our curly friend. Or maybe he just hid it well. Jerry's upbringing involved years of antiquated coddling and a family setting that made every failure a chance at earning love, affection, and celebratory comeuppance. He came out of childhood as a good person, but you simply cannot fix something by throwing money and sweet words at it. Thus, there are times that his untouched social stunting becomes so painfully prevalent that we cannot do anything except shake our heads and bear the embarrassment with him.

We all parted ways and it was a sunny afternoon when I arrived home. The house seemed a bit cleaner, a bit homelier, and, in my mind, a bit more colorful. It was as if I were wearing a new pair of glasses, or if I had just awoken from a lengthy sleep, one not inundated with the burden of too much deep slumber, almost invariably resulting in the distant, throbbing headache that lasts far too long into the waking hours.

I went to the kitchen and poured myself a glass of water from the tap. For a moment, I considered what exactly went into making our first world's water clean. How many added chemicals were there, what did they mean by added minerals, why were said minerals not present in the first place, and what led to the realization that we needed the minerals? Water is water. It is our baseline standing, a source of our livelihood. It makes up however much of our bodies and even more of our planet and we claim to understand that we can add x amount of y to make it "better," to make to make it more acceptable. To make the purest form of our existence purer. Playing God by claiming his toys are not good enough.

It is a simple glass. A cylinder a few inches tall and capable of shattering at a height of eighteen inches or more, chipping at twelve inches, and rolling with a thud at anything less. This glass belongs to set of utensils and home furnishings that my parents received as a wedding gift from some local businessman they were friends with, years ago, back before I was officially a bastard. I could remove dozens of plates and drink-ware from said matching set and arrange them, from practicality to size, through all varying degrees of use shown throughout. Oddly enough, since my parents were out-of-the-bottle alcoholics, the glassware was not the most worn products, but, in fact, the least touched.

In my mind, they spring up along my counter top: fifteen ceramic plates, eight glasses like the one in my hand, ten large dinner plates, dozens of utensils, a mixing bowl, a serving bowl, and a napkin holder. I hold up the glass in my hand to my eye and stare into the slightly bubbled tap water. Chemical influence and natural resistance, all by the hand of man, playing the hand of God, acting through one nation, under itself. The all-knowing being with an Oedipus complex.

Through the pale blue glass of water, I see something move through three layers of glass. Through the two sides of the cup and water, through the window, and through my backyard, I see people walking through the woods. I am instantly reminded of the incident involving my air conditioner, but it is only that nature club taking its stroll through the woods, once again. I am taken back to my high school days, when I, too, was a fan of the outdoors. On a day like today, they had the right idea. I finished the rest of my water, the imaginary plates having already disappeared, and go to look for my shoes.

The woods behind my house are dense. I am not sure if I have ever given much consideration to them. There were, at one point, plans to develop this land. There are acres of abandoned farmland after about a mile of forest. Beyond the trees, the land stretches, barren and brown, for what seems like forever. Objectively, three-fourths of a mile away, the forest begins once more, stretches for three miles, and then meets the shore. I am not sure if anywhere else in America could replicate Deptford's unique nature. Anywhere else, the shoreline properties would be scooped up and manhandled by their respective developers. Here, in Washington, it is far too rocky and steeply inclined to build any retirement or starter homes.

It does not take me long to remember what I had been missing and why I had originally enjoyed it. In the distance, a bird chirps happily. Invariably, a squirrel somewhere is getting its rocks off hiding some little discarded piece of nothing. I follow the hikers that I spotted from my window only loosely. As far as I know, the trail only goes for about two miles in this direction. What objective they had in these woods, I could only guess. But I suppose that mystery is all you could truly ask for and seek today. You cut off civilization from the wilderness and society will only seek to reclaim that wild frontier.

I have a half-empty bottle of water when I decide to take a seat. I must have walked for about twenty-five minutes and realized that my consumption of water would be much too frequent if I was stranded on a desert island. I take a seat on a fallen log that is conveniently placed on the side of the trail. I am staring up at the sun through the thick, green leaves of Deptford County, when a pretty, young voice calls out to me.

"Hi there!"

I am torn from my dazing. A young girl is standing there in the black windbreaker synonymous with the nature association.

"Uh, hello," I offer a half-hearted wave.

"What are you up to?" she asks, approaching, taking a seat on my log, only a few feet away.

"Just walking. I live in one of the houses back that way."

"Oh," she nods. "We do this every weekend."

"I know."

I recognize her from somewhere, but cannot exactly place it.

"Are you interested in protecting the forests?"

"Not particularly."

"Oh," she seemed defeated.

"Hey," I tried to cheer her up. "I actually ran a conservation club back in high school."

"Wow, did you live around here?"

"Pretty much all my life."

"Wait..." her eyes got all wide. "Are you Kevin—" I am withholding my last name for my own reasons.

"Yes."

"Oh my lord... no fucking way! TOM!" she called out to the woods.

"Wait, I—"

At this point a few more people came from the woods.

This was the rest of her hiking crew. These were the poor schmucks who went walking in my backyard every weekend, looking for some sort of salvation. The one I assumed to be "Tom" was a decent looking guy, a few years older than me, probably early thirties. He was just a little over average weight, but not heavy-set by any means. He had a very mild scar on his left cheek, most likely from adolescent acne, but was not blemished by any other noticeable childhood blight.

He, too, wore the black windbreaker synonymous with the organization and upon seeing the small woman with the colored hair sitting on the log, moved towards her, in protection or greeting, I could not tell. He only offered a brief greeting.

"Hello, stranger!"

The girl rose and countered.

"Tom, this is Kevin—" at the mention of my name, Tom's face went blank and he spun around, looking to the other morons who were walking with him. There were probably about ten of them, in all. If they wanted to mug me, they certainly could have. But, briefly scanning the group, they would never want to. They were a lot of middle-aged cashiers, pharmacists, and librarians. Those content in jobs that they would never wish to retire as, but never really bearing the motivation to seek anything more.

"How do you do?" Tom finally spoke, crossing to me and shaking my hand.

"I'm fine," I nodded. "Just walking a bit."

"Of course," Tom finally smiled. "Are you familiar with our group's recent work?"

"Not at all."

"We're the Deptford County Conservation Society. We—" I laughed and interrupted his prepared introduction.

"Oh, excuse me. I don't mean to be rude. Just, that was the name of my club in high school." The girl with colorful hair nodded, too eagerly, to my right. Tom cut in.

"Oh… you went to Deptford County Regional?"

"You know it."

"Sir, I think our group is an extension of your project," the girl said.

I rose and thought this through.

"Mr. Tom," I rose and looked this man in the eye. "If this is true…" I looked around the group. They were quite the motley crew. One of them was clearly beyond seventy years old. Certainly shouldn't have been hiking. "Then I pity your existence."

I started walking away and then it hit me. I spun around, walked towards the girl sitting on the log on put my hands on her shoulders.

"Oh, you!" I said. "Of course, you are the girl who works at the convenience store."

This was the girl who Jerry had unsuccessfully hit on a few months ago. The minor in a Star Wars shirt.

"Yes… yes, I do," she nodded, smiling.

I looked her up and down. She was now wearing a Goonies shirt, underneath the jacket.

"…Look into the nursing internship at the hospital, dearie," I turned and walked back towards my house.

The group was silent as I walked away from them, sucking water from my crumpled bottle.

CHAPTER TWENTY

On the way back towards my house, I think about what just unfolded, regarding the club. How far did its influence reach after I left Deptford for my stint at the state university? It could not have been too incredible, right? I mean, I left it to a bunch of nobodies working go-nowhere jobs reaching maybe a dozen people a week. Did it go viral? I smirk for a moment, considering the fact that the most forgettable legacy of my high school career became a lifestyle for people living in my hometown. This comforts me for a few minutes of my walk and then I think of Mariah.

In my mind, I can see and feel her walking next to me. She is not the decrepit, water-logged copy, or the adolescent version. She is exactly how she would have been, would she have grown up with us, normally. She is beautiful, she is always beautiful, and she walks on my left. She wears the black windbreaker of the club over a tank-top, and a pair of white cotton shorts. I am accompanied by a man I do not immediately recognize, but rationalize as my grandfather, and something is off. He walks on my right and is in full military garb. He wears an olive green uniform with medals adorning his chest. He looks just like pop, but something is different. His breathing is slightly stinted, but he does not make an ordeal of it.

We walk for another few minutes in silence. This is not terrifying to me. I enjoy it. Bask in it, even. Perhaps this man is an elderly relative and I am sharing a Sunday stroll with my wife, you know, the wife that would never be. After a few minutes, the old man has to stop. He unbuttons his shirt and rubs his bare chest. I look at Mariah and she smiles at me, those big eyes glittering in the loose sunbeams that manage to stab through the treetops. The old man struggles to his feet, buttons his shirt and takes a deep breath in.

"Sorry, son," he grits. "You know how it is."

Well, I don't, but we continue.

The world is beautiful here. Although I am within a mile of home, surely, I feel like I am a continent away. A few feet away from the path, in either direction, the vegetation is fringed in purple edges of a palette unknown to me. The dirt turns to sand in various places and bits of crystal sparkle in the sun, pieces of sand in dirt, a shoreline miles away from any ocean. I find little sublime comforts in these, but my companions do not pay any mind to them. We continue walking, as if we are dropping the old man off somewhere.

Soon enough, my offhanded descriptions manifest themselves and we find ourselves in a clearing. The trees fall away and the path dies, leaving us in a wide open field. The landscape rises and falls all around, forever rimmed by the treeline. In the center, the utmost center, a large hill rises and a small castle sits on it. I say "castle" because anything else would be a bastardization. It is truly a castle, done in the medieval style, one you would imagine to find in Ireland or England, the ones that they would sell "ghost tours" for an outrageous fee to young Americans on vacation.

It is beautiful and relatively small. A woman in a white uniform sits at its entry. We climb the hill without much effort and move to greet her. The old man in our party is not encumbered by the rolling expanse of the field. He is eager to get to our destination. As we approach, the nurse winks at me and nods to my companions. The old man, stopping for a moment, salutes the woman and then shakes her hand. He turns to me, something forever wrong with his person, and proceeds to shake my hand. Were I to objectively evaluate this coming moment, I should have punched him, flat out, but I do not. After he shakes my hand, he moves to Mariah and kisses her, deeply. She arches her back and he bends with her, in a completely stereotypical war-time era kiss, dipping her back, far, his old, disgusting tongue deep in her mouth, and she is loving every moment of it. I hear a small murmur of delight in her inflections and clear my throat, irritated.
The old man returns them to their standing position and Mariah blushes, turning away. The man smiles sheepishly and claps me on the shoulder, the bastard. He then speaks, a weak voice, looking forward to something.
"Kevin… until next time,"
The old fuck moves towards the entrance of the castle.

Before I can do anything, the iron grating of the archway begins falling, removing any possibility of entrance. I hazard a half-hearted "Wait!" but it is of no use. The nurse merely shakes her head slightly, her eyes closed and looking at the ground. She is happy with whatever just happened, but offers me no explanation.

"Pop, wait!" I rattle the gate, but no one answers. I turn and shake the woman, but she is only giggling and looking towards the ground.

Mariah pulls at me, gently pleading, offering nothing but, "Kevin, please," and tugs at my elbow. Even in this Valhalla of discontent, I do not comfort my Mari, even in this limbo which I have unfettered access to the woman I love, I do not go to console her. I am rattling the cage of a castle that may or may not exist, disregarding her well-being. Eventually, the hillside begins bleeding an oversaturation of color. The contours and lines of the landscape begin ebbing and warping into a confused state of tangibility. The black lines of the space explode and leak their ink all over this canvas. The green hills and grey castle become inseparable and I can no longer see.

I feel Mariah pulling me from behind, her gentle hands on both of my elbows, tugging at me, desperately trying to get me away from the gate. She is saying my name.

"Kevin…" her voice echoes.

"Kevin…" Sara says from somewhere, far away.

"Kevin!" Sara pleads.

I open my eyes. I am laying on my side in my backyard, a few feet away from my small patio area. Bleeding hearts of the world, kill me. Smother me in my sleep. Mother fucker. I close my eyes again for a moment, desperately trying to again, once more, see the hillside and the castle. It is gone. The old man and my love are gone. Instead, I am in my backyard with my second-rate source of reliability and a propane-fueled grill.

CHAPTER TWENTY-ONE

Sara takes me inside and pours me a glass of water. She has been going on and on about these little sleeping spells for about twenty minutes now. She is asking herself, when will they stop, what is causing them, can medicine help or is my medicine causing it, and a dozen other questions that neither her or I could ever hope to adequately address. She is glancing at her cell phone and mumbling to herself. She looks up.

"Dr. Mason's office is probably closed for the afternoon already."

"Okay," I reply.

"We can talk to her about this. She did hint at the possibilities of you acting up a few days before you came to," Sara says, rubbing her shoulders.

"I do not think she is allowed to release that kind of information to you," I mutter.

"I was the only dumbfuck in the room with you for nearly the entire time, Kevin," Sara spits. "A month is a long time, be thankful that it wasn't fucking Jerry who was recording your medications and how much—"

"Oh, leave him out of this. Christ," I roll my eyes.

"Okay," Sara breathes in. "I'm sorry. It's just really, really nerve-wracking to not know if you'll wake up in the same place I see you go to sleep. I don't want you getting hurt when you're delirious."

"I understand," I stare out the window. "I do appreciate it. But don't worry about it. We can call her tomorrow."

"Alright."

The next day we do just that. Rather, Sara does just that. I am reading an article about a private space shuttle endeavor online at my desk when she peeks her head into the kitchen, the phone to her ear.

"Kevin," she asks. "Can you drop by the office around three to pick up your prescription?"

I audibly moan and throw my arms up in false-protest and she smiles.

"Yes, doctor, that will be fine," she disappears behind the wall. "Are you sure you don't need a consultation? No—it's common after trauma like that? Alright, then, he'll swing by later. Thank you."

I almost want to ask if Sara can go and pick it up for me, but I realize that she has work in an hour. My mouth that was open moments ago to ask her of this favor slowly draws shut, ridiculed by my own self-hate and thoughts of a self-image debased. I should really be actively seeking employment instead of reading about men whose footsteps I shall never trod in on a stupid website online, but, alas. So long as the state keeps sending these buffering checks, I am in no rush. I am the recovering inebriant bent on sapping all I can from the system, or so the conservative mainstream media would have you believe.

A little while later, Sara kisses me on my head and says she'll see me later, after work. I shout a goodbye after her and almost fall out of my chair when I remember something: I can't drive.

"Fuck!" I spin and fall. "Sara!"

I get up and rush to the door, but she is already halfway down the block. God damn it. I really do not want to bother either of the guys, so I call Mitch. Per his nature, he tells me, "of course, I'll see you soon," and we leave it at that. On the car ride there, I ask him, "how's the Swede?" and he promises that he has no idea what I mean. I guess they are bitter about the nickname. The ride there is only ten or so minutes anyway. I pick up my prescription, stare at one of the nurse's backsides as they lead a patient into a screening room (nothing to write home about) and promptly leave.

Mitch offers to take me to the pharmacy and I thank him. He waits outside and smokes a cigarette. I consider teasing him about it but he seems to be in a bad mood so I let it go. I nod to an old man behind the register and walk towards the back, to the actual pharmacy portion of the convenience store. A value as constant as night and day, the tall pharmacist is back there. The man with dark skin and white teeth is adjusting something out of sight, behind his computer's display, and upon noticing me, smiles and says, "Hello, sir."

"Hello," I take the blue piece of paper out of my pocket and uncrumple it towards him. "I need this to be filled out, please."

He smoothes out the paper on the plastic counter and reads the hastily scribbled words to himself. For a moment, his head still leaning down towards the paper, he looks up at me, judging something. He flattens out the script once more and takes it from the counter, turning, "Of course, let me check." My usual procedure for this is involves dropping it off and returning a few hours or days later, once they receive it in the mail or whatever delivery system they have for medication. Maybe today's my lucky day.

I suppose it is. He returns with your typical orange twist-off bottle of medication, complete with directions, in a sealed plastic bag. I notice the faintest trace of blue residue on his gloves from the procurement transaction, so I hypothesize that this medication is simply a revamping of my former dosage. I hand him my insurance information and credit card and he glances at the computer monitor. He doesn't charge me and insists that it's covered. He simply scans my insurance on a device below the counter and returns my cards. I shrug at this modern nicety and thank him. I quickly glance at his nametag and thank him by his name, "Thank you, Art." He simply smiles and nods once, returning to his previous work.

As I turn to walk down the aisle and back towards the entrance. I spot a "Community Events!" bulletin board near a hall cutting towards the restrooms. The obnoxious colors and decoration of the piece draws my attention and I find slight pleasure in the menagerie of various depictions of our town's mascot, Lenny, celebrating the upcoming fair. Although I smile at the sight of the whimsical creature, I am also slightly repulsed by the force-fed mimetic nature of this damned carnival. It is the only thing that the sad, sad people around Deptford County are talking about and it seems that as the week-long event draws closer, the more and more idiots there are in the streets talking about it.

Another bit that I am unprepared for is an advertised "wine-tasting extravaganza" – but perhaps, after reading more on the flyer, I shouldn't have been so eager to be disappointed. It is hosted by "Deptford County's Very Own Salvatore Delange, Connoisseur." Apparently, this is an annual event, filled with "art, theatre, good wine, and good friends" in preparation for the big event (the county fair). I chuckle and tear off one of the little RSVP slips. I avert my eyes and prepare to exit. With one last glance towards the pharmacy counter, I see Art writing something on a clipboard.

His professionalism is unmatched. His grace and candor is unlike anything else you will find paid by the hour in the Western world. His unyielding precision belongs only in that of the realm of a politician or a surgeon, and to that measure, he disgusts me.

CHAPTER TWENTY-TWO

Mitch drives me home. He is much more solemn than usual. Of all the words I could have ever used to describe the man, I would never have fingered "solemn" was one of them. Cheerful, loyal, helpful, never a downer. Then again, I do tend to have that effect on people. I do not know whether to smirk or frown upon this realization, that I diminished this man's personality. I, instead, roll down the window. He offers to take "the scenic route" and I nod, not having any other plans.

We take the coastal highway. We will end up going about twenty minutes out of the way, making the ten minute trip a half-hour adventure. At one point, at the crest of a long, sloping arc in the curve of the road, we pull over and stop. The winding highway sits atop a wide-array of mountainous elevation over varying severities of oceanic drops and rough surfs. Where we pull over, there is about twenty yards of dirt and pebbles, a metal guardrail, and a fifty foot drop onto rocks below. We sit on the guardrail for a moment and breathe in the salty air.

Across the void from us, the cliffs and road begins again, continuing the wide U-shape parting from our right. There is a solid eighth of a mile of open air between us and the other side, but you can see it, clear as day, even under these ever-present clouds. Beyond the other side of the road are miles of forest. Even further, the hills reclaim the land we can see an assisted living home on the top of one of these minor mountains, overlooking both the woods and coastal roads. Countless blends of green and browns smear this landscape, disturbed only by the persistent shadings of grey and white, permanently cast by the stone and the sky that keep us chained to this stretch of earth.

I wonder to myself exactly how many old souls live cooped up in that building, contained behind walls of concrete, their only companions the salaried caregivers and the other invalids, discarded by society, even worse-off than themselves. If I ever reach that point, euthanize me. As if reading my mind (or perhaps just following my gaze) Mitch speaks up.

"I used to work there," he nods and points at the building a few miles away on the hill.

"Yeah?"

"Yes, just out of high school. I would clean the patient's beds and feed them. Play cards with them. Just that kind of low-end healthcare job."

"Did you like it?"

He breathes in and weighs the question.

"Honestly… no. I enjoyed helping them. I liked being there for them. It was just far too toxic of an environment though for a young person. If you had even one, normal friend or relative on the outside, you could not imagine living like these poor people. Their families, or the state, whoever was responsible for them, would deem them too unstable to take care of at home and lock them up in the castle until they died. So, no. I did not like it. Seeing them smile made it worthwhile, but there were just too many blank stares to make up for it." He discards the cigarette that I did not notice he was holding.

"Jeez." I deadpan. He laughs.

"Yeah, I know. But hey, you asked." We both change our sceneries and look down into the water. "I used to drive all the way down here on my lunch breaks, though. Well, actually, over there." He points to the other side of the curve. "Yup, would throw rocks off the cliff and eat out of my brown bag. Kids who were still in high school would drive by in their trucks and call me 'faggot' out the window. But hey, look who's laughing." Another chuckle.

"Sorry, dude," I offer.

"Oh, please," he waved me away. "They were high school fucks. They're probably doing the same thing we are now… well, same thing I am. You, you're kind of a Deptford success story. Well, at least before the whole—"

"Yeah." I was a hero until I got drunk and drove off of a bridge.

"Why'd you come back?"

"Mitch, I never left. I just never socialized with all those circles of people who were only ever looking to backstab one another with the next piece of personal news and bullshit. I was always here. Instead of renting a house with a few buddies, I lived in my grandma's house. Instead of moving to where the big money and technology was, I fucking commuted. I never returned from the hero lifestyle, I rejected it."

This little outburst created a smug little look on my mouth and a smug little explosion of ego and dopamine in my body. I felt proud with my little rant. Mitch stepped on his cigarette on the ground and twisted his foot, silencing the ember.

"You know, Kevin," Mitch said, rising and turning to get back into the car. "For being the smartest guy I know, you sure are fucking stupid."

CHAPTER TWENTY-TWO

For the duration of the ride home, we sit in silence. We do take a few more detours around the coastal highway and he ends up driving past the assisted living home and through the woods. It is an odd time of day, just before the sun sets, but long since you could trace its path in the sky. The trees create a twilight of their own and the mist is what carries the light, not some celestial being, not a star or a moon, but the water in the air defies purposes and blots our visual palette, replacing depth and distance with hues of gray and smoky clouds that conjure the word "precipitation" on the back of our tongues.

We drive along the base of the big hill, the sprawling concrete structure consuming the entirety of the summit and the inorganic lights are soft orange embers burning in a damp world. It has not heavily rained in a few days, but the ground is still wet wherever you look. Cascadia is an ethereal place manifested on earth and our beloved state of Washington brings out its beauty in the most unseen, untouched places, going from point A to B. There exists no Valhalla, no Atlantis, no Heaven, no Valley of the Gods in our reality, but surely you can find sublimity in the undeveloped portions of the Pacific Northwest. I find myself lamenting the lack of connection to my roots as the car pushes on.

Mitch asks me about the tab of paper I mentioned when I had initially re-entered the vehicle. I told him about the wine party and he laughed. Apparently, it was all Sal had been talking about that week. He had actually asked Mitch if he should extend an official invitation my way, but was too nervous and reluctant to act. I told him that I was not terribly excited to take part in such an event, but would gladly do it, if only for the free booze. Mitch went on to describe the formalities of wine tasting, but I ignored them. Those who spend time spitting out good wine will be the first against the walls when I am king.

He drops me off and I thank him for the favor. It really meant a lot to me, that whole bit. I get inside and sit. A woman spins a wheel on the television. A man sells me laundry detergent on the television. I watch a young couple get married and murdered on the television and then Sara comes home.

I rise and greet her at the door. I kiss her on the neck, the cheek, and then her lips. She warms up to me immediately and wraps her arms around my neck. She is not accustomed to these affections. Nor am I. We sit and talk for a while in the kitchen. Although she is one of my stoutest sobrietors, she has no objections when we open a bottle of the expensive whiskey and bitch about the people in our lives. I tell her about Sal's wine party. I do not tell her about Mitch's favor and chauffeuring, but she tells me she thinks it would be fun if we went. The next morning, I will call Sal and respond to the flyer. That night, Sara and I do the deed and I sleep a dreamless sleep.

For once in my life, everything seems normal. I am not visited by spectres and visions of my past. I am not accosted by regret at every drop of a hand, at every lift of a limb, at every extension of a muscle. Sara is more than onboard for the wine tasting, which turns out to be a masquerade party. I do not really care, but it is nice to have the people in your life excited for something for once in their collective existence. News of this function has caught onto Jerry and Ted, and although Ted is not interested, Jerry sees this as the perfect opportunity to strut his recently-found courage. Jerry, his new girlfriend, Millie, Sara, and I are all registered as attendees at Sal's wine-tasting social.

The evening before the event, Ted sends me a text message on my phone. I am in the bathroom, my dress shirt hanging on the door behind me, staring at me through the mirror, when my phone vibrates. It reads, "Tell me how it goes with ole goomba, okay?" He is obviously talking about Jerry. He is obviously talking in the hushed tone and shared secrecy of friends within a group of friends. I write half a dozen drafts of text messages before I finally close my phone and do not respond at all. Any further progress is only hindering the love of another trusted companion. Ted does not mean any harm, but I cannot help but to feel the venom in his words. Is this the impression I leave on people?

We all meet at my house the night of the event at five pm. I have always hated this feeling. The event is not until eight pm, yet everyone is at my house, all dressed and ready to go, just after five. We have three hours to kill, filling the halls of my grandmother's house. The only thing missing is our parents taking the pre-prom pictures and embarrassing us all to unbearable oblivion. I hate it. I want to hide in the bathroom, although I am among friends. I want to tear off the stupid fucking tie hanging from my neck, remove my jacket, and just take a walk in the woods. I want to put headphones on, turn on music, and be a recluse for yet another night. But no, I have to be social. It is that undying pang of anxiety and discomfort that was cultivated sometime before your fifth birthday, that first resonation that told you that you were out of place when you did something embarrassing in public. Our toddler minds never felt it and we certainly did not know it as infants, nor will we know it as crippled elders when our minds have festered and soiled into sad, sodden, useless things. But once you are capable of thought, a sensation more primal and influential than physical danger took precedence.

This is what civilization does once it becomes too efficient. No, this is what people do when their survival rate becomes too solidified. Take the danger out of society and we'll create a new organic fear, an anxiety to match the times.

Jerry and Millie, well, they are obviously a little bit more than normal framed. They are visibly overweight. But they do look very dapper in their formal wear and plastic, faux-porcelain masks. Millie, bless her soul, is wearing a pink dress, hemmed in black and crimson, and a wide theatre mask. Jerry, the fuck, is wearing a black suit with a crimson tie. His mask is the glistening face of a rabbit, complete with ears and ridiculous eyebrows. I must admit, it looks awesome in the light. Maybe I am just envious that the portly couple pulled it off so well.

To that extent, Sara does look amazing, as well. Her thin body is wrapped in a tight black dress, like an exoskeleton or an Egyptian wrap, covering her torso and upper thighs and that is all. Her frail shoulders and arms are exposed, as are her legs. The dress is black and lace and absolutely stunning. We all look good, the motley lot of us. Hell, even I would say that I was dressed nicely. I donned my faux-porcelain mask (a goat-like rendition, presumably of the deity, Pan) and we all took a picture, reflected in the living room mirror. Sara wore a generic theatre mask and her frame, frozen there as the half-lives of the camera's flash died away, was breathtaking. She was gorgeous tonight. I had let her know this as we had "celebrated" the fact in the bathroom before Millie and Jerry arrived.

It was held at the community center. Everything was held at the community center, but "everything" includes exponential bullshit, from girl scout meetings to town hall discussions to fundraisers. You know, things I could not bother myself to care about. I realized as we signed in at the front desk and entered the gymnasium-like hall, that this was the very room where a younger Sal had taken a photo with my grandfather a few decades earlier. This is where that photograph on his computer was born. I get distracted at this thought and my party starts moving on without me. I am picturing the rows of folding chairs, the small easel with the photo display, and the smiling faces.

Would you know, it is like a reunion of people who have no business in my life. Walt's widow is here, too. She is stationed at the water table, sitting next to dozens of small paper cups, three-quarters filled with water from a large plastic jug. For her sake, she's sitting. Her arthritic knees would inevitably give out otherwise. She looks all done up, like you would imagine a grandmother in her Sunday best: a faded pink blouse, a long dark skirt, a drooping knitted hat, and a crocheted pink shawl. Her eyes wander the hall without much sentience, but she offers a friendly twitch of the mouth, a quarter-smile, when she momentarily stops her gaze on me. I smile and raise my hand a bit to wave, but her eyes are already elsewhere.

I see local business owners. I see some of the older staff from Dr. Mason's practice. I see a grocer, I see the convenience store manager, I see Art from the pharmacy. They are all contained in their little respective bubbles of conversation throughout the room. Salvatore looks like the Monopoly guy, flitting from table to table across the room, his coattails dancing like a cape. There are probably about a dozen of these tables set up, with the appropriate bottles of wine and tasting cups and napkins and that whole bit. The room does smell lovely with this many open bottles. Sara is talking to a group of people our age. When they notice me, they all wave past Sara, but are already whispering to her in hushed judgment by the time I look away. Millie and Jerry do not really know what to do with themselves. Millie told us that her parents would be attending as well, so I assume she was anxiously awaiting their arrival, in order to anchor their presence to someone besides the vacant space of the floor. Jerry doesn't know what to do with his arms.

Sal hovers over to me and I move to shake his hand. He takes it, kisses it, and moves in for a hug. He has a large, ornate, dragonfly-like mask over his glasses. The imp is literally about a foot shorter than me, I realize. He was never this close. He smells like lilac and toothpaste. "How are you, Kevin!"

"I'm fine, Sal," we disengage from the embrace. "We all just got here." I loosely point towards my dispersed party. Sal smiles and waves at Jerry and Millie.

"Oh, don't they look nice!"

"Yes," I said. "We don't dress up much. Jer really cleans up well, huh?"

"Oh, well, he's your friend, I guess you would know better than me," Sal laughs.

We stand there for a few moments. Sal is smiling with his mouth half-open, as if he was listening to me speak. But I'm just standing there, feeling like I should be holding a drink, waiting for him to either say something or pixie-float away somewhere else. Eventually, he clears his throat.

"Well, my dearest Kevin, we should be getting started shortly," he removes his mask and glances down at a pocket watch. It catches a loose sparkle of light in the dim hall and it looks to be a beautiful piece of machinery. Or would it be jewelry? "Have fun, children!"

I crack my neck and shrug my shoulders, trying to ease this bit of tension that had just came about. The couple move back towards me. Millie stares after Sal.

"You know Mr. Delange?" Millie asks. It is odd hearing him being referred to as anything but "Sal."

"Yes," I reply. "More or less. I did some computer work for him. He was a friend of that guy Mitch's and… yeah. That's how I know him."

"Oh," she says. "He's like the mayor of Deptford. I remember him throwing these parties since I was a little girl. I mean you can even ask my—"

Millie was going to say "mother" but instead let out an excited little shrill that gave birth to the inklings of a migraine in the back of my eyes. She scurries away from Jerry and I and my eyes focus in on an older couple who had just walked through the door. The woman is essentially Millie, plus forty pounds and twenty years. The man is a burly figure who conjures images of cigarette commercials from the nineties and makes you recall watching episodes of This Old House with your father, not understanding the appeal of watching people practice construction and architecture. They must hail from somewhere out east. They are both in Southern garb, the man wearing a blue cowboy shirt with white trimmings. I do not think they know what "masquerade" means.

"Go get 'em, tiger," I pat Jerry on the shoulder and he stumbles over to introduce himself. I smile after them and close my eyes for a second. This isn't so terrible.

Sal gives an introductory speech and people clap as he finishes up, wishing us health and good fortune as we get closer to the fair. I notice that many of the tables have little papier-mâché Lennies on them, the awkward manatee abortion, on a nest of floral arrangements. The room is dark and serene. The warm glow of the candles on the tables are expertly placed (by Sal, I'm sure) and maroon and purple rice-paper partitions are blocking lamps in the corners of the room and gives the entire scene a warm, night-by-the-sea ambience.

I was surprised when I first saw them, but remembering how small my world is, shouldn't have been when we met up with Mitch and the Swede. I wasn't a jerk to him tonight and we all enjoyed ourselves. Millie, Jerry, Mitch, and the Swede. We were a power group, acting as Sal's guinea pigs to demonstrate proper technique and whatnot to rest of the community. At one gleaming moment tonight, the Swede tried one flavor on Sal's recommendation and milled it about for a few seconds after sampling it. He smiled and pointed to me, "Kevin, I think you would like this one." He leaned the bottle in my direction and Mitch stared at me with wide eyes. I smiled, obliged, and let him pour for me. Mitch sighed happily, the Swede grinned, and Jerry whispered why this was a big deal to Millie, excusing them and taking her hand and walking away, towards her parents. The tension was gone, at last. Well, at least publicly. You know me.

I was never into the idea of wine tasting, but this is enjoyable. I decide after about three more samples in that this is the equivalent of masturbating until you're almost there and then going to bed, so I fill a glass with a red that I liked and retreat to the outer ring of the tables, content in my tasting, and settling for straightforward drinking. I realize at this point that I was on my own for almost an hour. Mitch and the Swede were talking to Sal across the room and Jerry was making inroads with Millie's father. By the gesturing of his arms, I assume they were either talking about football or skinning a deer. I glance up at the clock on the wall and see that we had been here for quite a while now. Where the hell did Sara and her group get to?

Images of high school events flash behind my eyes. Visuals of her being stupid burn into my retinas. I feel an emptiness in my stomach that is just as quickly replaced by a leaden weight. I scan the room. I do not see her or her friends from the area. I do not see the three guys she was talking to, or the four girls. You know, high school ends, but people never grow up. I clutch my drink and move towards the exit. A lady in a sweater tells me I am not allowed to take that, referring to the wine, outside. I drop the metal cup and the purple liquid explodes up the side of my pant leg and all over the white tile in the foyer. She stands up and exclaims, but I am already outside.

The front of the building is dark and the sidewalk to the parking lot is empty. I look around the yard and hear giggling from around the corner. I move across the wet grass and round the corner to see the unlit side of the building. Voices and laughter are coming from the back. Stumbling and bracing against the brick wall every few paces I clear the length of the building and see a handful of shadowed figures standing around. Immediately in front of me, a ball of sparks illuminates the scene from the mouth of a lighter. A girl in a navy blue dress, the figure right in front of me, smokes pot from a glass pipe. Behind her, a guy and a girl giggle and push each other, shoulder to shoulder, waiting for their hit from the bowl. Beyond them, Sara is backed against the wall, one leg wrapped around some guy, his hand up the back of her dress, squeezing her ass. Their tongues are in each other's mouths.
"What the fuck, Sara."
The three schmucks in front of me are fixated on the weed. Sara doesn't hear me over the sound of sucking face.
"Excuse me."
The circus of the flying fucks continues.

I grab the pipe from the girl in front of me and she protests. Her two friends are staring at me in the dark. Sara is still preoccupied. The girl with the lighter says, "If you wanted a hit, you could have just asked—" and hands me the lighter. I turn and heave the lighter across the field in the darkness and, changing the weight of the pipe in my hands, turn and pitch the glass bowl at the side of the brick building.

"What the fuck, man?" the guy who was looking forward to a hit pushes towards me.

"Get the fuck off of me," I spit. He continues towards me and I am moving towards Sara. He wants to fight, so I engage him, clutching his hair behind his ear. I slam his head into the wall and he collapses, clutching the injury. The girl screams and starts hitting me. The girl who was holding the lighter is still staring after it.

"Hey, what's the fucking problem?"

The guy Sara was kissing is facing me and adjusts his belt. Sara is meek and shrinks behind him. She has been caught. The man she is with does not understand the ramification of my presence. I stand there, breathing, angry, clenching my fists. A sharp pain stabs into my brain, but I blink it off. The wine that was delicious moments ago, the remainder of my glass which is now in the foyer, feels as if its residue is burning my tongue. My eyes have been adjusting to the dark. I can see Sara's eyes. I can see her makeup begin to run. She's crying a bit, but not sobbing. I know they're bloodshot. I know she's high off her ass. She's probably drunk, too. I want to hit her, but I would never.

I want the guy to hit me. I want the lot of them to kick the ever-loving shit out of me. But they won't.

I breathe in.

I let go of my fists.

I close my eyes.

I let go of my visible rage.

"Don't come home tonight," I say.

"Please."

I sit on a bench in the foyer and watch a janitor mop my mess up from before. The lady in the sweater stares at me angrily. I stare back at her for a little while. Light orchestral music plays from inside. Sometimes it alternates to smooth jazz. Sal, master of ceremonies, even slips a few contemporary hits on and then some more classics. Hotel California comes on and I decide that I have rehabilitated enough.

Mitch comes to me, knowing. Sara must have whined to him, probably over the phone, even though they were only separated by a wall of brick. He pats me on the shoulder and asks how I'm doing.

"You know I've been used to it," I stare past him. "Just don't like actually seeing it."

He nods.

"Hey," he points to an unopened bottle. He gives a thumbs up and I nod. The party has ceased being a wine tasting and has broken into a collective conversational get-together, with a few sparse couples slowly dancing around the extremities.

"No point in letting it go to waste, eh?" he pours me a glass. Because, you know, the best way to help an addict is to enable them.

With every glass I finish, the pain in my head burns more. I excuse myself to the restroom and take some of my medication. The pills always rub off and falter to a blue residue on my palms and fingertips when I handle them. I swallow four, blow the dust off, and rinse my hands in the sink. The fluorescent lighting flickers for a moment and I am alone in the stark-white tiled room. I sigh and return to the hall. Jerry doesn't know. Mitch is the only one here who knows why I am no longer smiling. They chalk it up to me being my usual douchebag self. But who are they to blame?

I talk a little bit more to Sal, to various acquaintances, to Jerry, and eventually Millie's parents. I want to go home. I want to sleep. The medicine isn't working, nor is the wine. Each sip furthers the pain. This isn't what I wanted.

CHAPTER TWENTY-THREE

I wake up at home. A message on my phone from Jerry informs me that Mitch and the Swede drove me home after I got sick at the party. They said I had blinding migraines and was sitting in the foyer, almost asleep. Well, at least I didn't make a fool of myself this time. Well, besides having Sara trading spit with that fuck out back. My head is heavy. I feel hung over, but I certainly did not drink to that level. What a way to live: waking day to waking day, strung together only by the connective fiber of a painkilling supplement that will not even fulfill its purpose.

After an hour of rolling around in bed, I get up, and take more of the useless medicine. Blue residue powders the entire top edge of my sink. It is in the crevices of the mirror, it is between the bristles of my toothbrush, it is under my eyes, on my sleeves, in my glass of water. I refuse to clean right now. I go and stare into my full refrigerator, which might as well be empty. I make a cup of coffee and stand at my living room window. It is cloudy out, and if I didn't have a significant other who didn't persistently betray my trust, I would suggest we stayed inside, watch favorite movies, and wait for the rain. Alas, here I am, standing in my boxers and open robe, staring at the street. The patch of forest to the left of the property sways with the unfelt, unheard wind. It will be a beautiful little storm, but as of yet, is just a gloomy promise.

I end up sinking into a chair, still staring outside, waiting for nothing. The coffee in my mug has slightly chilled. A significant amount of cream has loosed from the blend and sits on top of the liquid, undisturbed. Answering my unmade prayers, I spot a gray Oldsmobile gliding down the street towards my house. Even a block away, I know it's for me. Even a block away, I know that whoever is inside the vehicle wishes to bother me. I sigh and reluctantly get a t-shirt on under my robe. I did at least this much, whoever it was could deal with my visible underwear. I probably should have just put sweatpants on.

I watched Sal get out of his car after parking in my driveway and peer towards the doorstep. The number of the house was nailed just to the side of the doorknob and upon seeing it through his glasses; he reached back into his car, pulled out an overflowing folder of papers, and started waking up my driveway. Christ, what does he want? "Hello, Sal," I open the door to his raised fist, beating him to the knock.

"Oh, hello, Kevin," he smiled, looking up. "I wanted to bring you some things."

"How did you get my address?"

"It's a small world, come now!" he smiles. I do not appreciate whoever betrayed my address to Sal.

"Come in."

We sit in the living room and he declines any offer for a beverage. He tells me that he was on his way to run some errands when he decided to drop off a little "care package" to my house.

"I know you're cooped up here all the time," he said. "And with the weatherman saying we're supposed to have heavy rains for the next few days, I figured, well—" he hefted the stack of papers and folders. "I figured you might enjoy some reading material."

I knew what they were before he told me.

"They're my projects, Kevin,"

"Oh,"

"Yes, I've never shared my complete collection with anyone else. Of all your friends, Mitch has only read one or two. Sure, some of those folks from the party may have read one when I leave a stack at the community board or at the library, but none of them really know my artistic side."

"I," I begin. "Well, I appreciate that, Sal, really."

"Yes, yes, it's nothing, I swear. I love sharing with the young people."

He again looked at me, prepared to say something, but simply… stared. Waiting for me to start a conversation. Oh, how precious, you fool. How powerfully you do not know me.

"So, Kevin," he eventually began. "I heard that you and your lady had a little bit of a skirmish at the event last night…?"

Oh, you wily old cunt.

"Yes," I cleared my throat. "Yes, we did."

For once, his silent gaze was successful in pulling more words from my being.

"We don't... exactly have the most secure relationship. What am I saying, we're not really actually together—"

"And what constitutes being together, Kevin?" Sal asked.

"Well, we're not 'dating,' she doesn't consider me her 'boyfriend' and I don't consider her—"

"But she loves you, Kevin, does she not?"

Oh, stop it, you fuck.

"Yeah... well, she says she does. But then she's all over town, sucking—"

"Kevin, do you tell her you love her?"

"No. Because she's so distant from me all the time—" he literally cutting me off, every response I gave. I was useless.

"Well, do you see that the cycle is so apparent?"

I stared at the wall beyond Sal.

"She says she loves you. It's the 21st century, son, it's fine that you're not married, or in what you publicly label a relationship. Hell, you do not even have to call her anything beyond friend, or her name. But she says she loves you. You spend many evenings with her, no? And she helps with your whole... medical issues of recent? And you find it odd that she does not have a sense of stability in your wake?"

"Sal, you might be right... but you just don't understand, it has always been like that, since high school. She never grew up. She doesn't get out of the whole—"

"Kevin, you're claiming she is not mature enough to love, yet who here is talking about high school? I am almost three times your elder. Do you want to know a secret? You're right: people never grow up. But walking around like a smug juror wielding the secret to mankind, that – gasp! – people are immature does not make you wise. It paints you as the arrogant clown that no one wishes to associate with."

Jesus Christ, Sal.

I cleared my throat again and remained silent. I rubbed my hands together and began kneading my fingers and palms, feeling the tendons and muscle and bone, distracting myself. Inspecting the freckle on a finger, the dust on the carpet below, the light patches of hair on my bare feet. I even felt the early tremor of tears behind my eyes, but refused to yield that intimacy to Sal. I scratched my head and looked up, preparing a failed rebuttal, but he spoke first.

"Listen, Kevin," he began. "You are not a terrible person. I understand – I completely understand – that she may have wronged you in the past. But you are doing nothing to foster a positive outcome. What is your endgame? Do you love her or not?"

I blinked. He continued.

"You have two options, and two options only. Then again, this is only advice. You only have these options for your happiness and your sanity's sake, from my point of view. But what do I know? I'm just an old trembling spinster writing plays!" He chuckled and rubbed his forehead. "You can either commit yourself fully and be the most loving man you can be to that troubled young woman who loves you so much -- I can see it. And she is a good person, Kevin. You have wronged her, too -- or, otherwise, you can leave her. Tell her you wish to cease further correspondence. You cannot sustain this. You are killing yourself and probably hurting others in the process. Please."

I had not noticed the plainness of his voice during this last bit of the lecture. After he laughed about his artistic nature, about writing plays, he became chillingly monotonous. He was not moving as he delivered those words. He was looking directly at me. We stared at each other for a few seconds. Then he smiled and broke the trance.

"Well, then, no more with that depressing business, eh?" he started leafing through his papers and I rolled my eyes.

"This one, A Mauve Assailant, is my personal favorite and I feel it's right up your alley. It's about a man who is destined for great things, but is such an utter fool when it comes to romance!"

"Jeez, Salvatore, thanks."

"Oh, you know I'm teasing you. But that's my quick synopsis. Oh, this one," he skips over a packet. "You already heard of the Yellowed King."

"Yes. Sal, was that based on anything?"

He sat up.

"Are you accusing me of plagiarism?"

"What? No, not at all. It's just... a popular story—"

"It's called an allusion, good lord, how many people in the drama club ridiculed me for it, the treasonous bastards—"

"Sal, dude, calm down. It's fine. I like it."

"Oh, okay. Well then."

"This one is called Black Heart, Blacker Medallion, and is about a crooked soldier."

All of these sounded like bad soap operas, or even worse, pornographic films.

A Professor Abroad, Don't Blink Upon a Reflection Broken, A Songbird Sings in Snow, Bloodied Daggers and the Rising Sun, Our Hero and Our Lord, Born Of the Stars, and, at last, Amongst Ashen Waste and Great Purpose.

"Wow, you sure were a prolific little creature, weren't you?"

If I had wanted to read all of these, it would last me until next spring.

"Oh, you flatter me."

I do not know if Sal knows what "prolific" means.

"Well, Kevin, I hope you enjoy them. I must be going. I spoke to young Mitch before. He told me he was going to try and help you settle things with Sara later, so expect a phone call or something in that manner from him or your lover."

I was going to protest, but I realized that Sal was only the messenger. A proverb would warn me not to shoot him and I suppose this bears truth, especially when they're an aging hipster man who cannot get enough of the theatre. He says goodbye and leaves, I half-heartedly read the cover pages of a few of the stories and fall onto the couch. I am laying with the side of my head down and staring out across my living room at the blank TV. I blink and it is early evening, amidst a formidable rainstorm. Hm.

A dull throbbing emits from the bags under my eyes and I am vividly reminded of the searing pain of last night. I am not in pain at the moment, but incredibly aware of where I was afflicted, as if they finally removed the knife that stabbed me and I am longing for its presence. Odd. I move to the bathroom and take my afternoon dosage. Every day, I fill a small plastic cube with four pills. I take two in the morning and I take two at night. Well, my box is empty. Perhaps in the excitement that Sal brought with him (if that is even the applicable word) I had forgotten to load the cartridge. No bother. I take two straight from the bottle and drink a glass of water. I feel refreshed, if only a little hungry.

I should probably call Sara. Or Jerry at least, to see how everything went after I got sick at the wine tasting party. I notice a dozen missed phone calls and messages on my phone, but clear the notifications. I'll get to them eventually. My finger hovers over Sara's name for a few moments, but I ultimately decide to call Jerry.

"Hey, Jerry,"

"Dude, Kevin?" he sounds frantic.

"Yes?"

"Oh, my god, Kevin. Everyone was worried sick, where have you been?"

"I was sleeping on the couch… Mr. Delange dropped off some reading material this morning and—"

"Kevin, Sara and Mitch told me that he dropped that stuff off on Sunday morning."

"And? It is Sunday, schmuck."

"Kevin, it's Thursday. Are you alright, man?"

I am stricken with a sense of syncope. Not since my accident have I felt so vulnerable, so out of place. Jerry kept talking through the phone.

"Sara said she stopped by that afternoon, but you were gone. I'll call her and let her know you're okay, but she's – well, we've all been – terrified, dude."

"No," I run a hand through my hair. "No, I'm fine, Jer. Thanks."

"Don't be surprised if Sara shows up tonight and drowns you in bony hugs," Jerry says, trying to comfort me.

"Noted," I say. "Thanks, dude."

"Bye."

I go to the bathroom and I vomit into the toilet.

Almost eighteen hours later, around midnight, Sara came in and we held each other. She apologized and I told her to shut up. Here's your modern apology. We slept.

"What is this shit, anyway?" Sara says, inspecting the bottle, pacing back and forth, her other hand holding the phone to her ear.

"I don't know, dear," I mumble. I am lying on the couch. My head hurts. "I am only the obliging patient."

"But it's fucking you up, badly," she cries. "Doctors are supposed to know what they're doing."

"There's a reason they call it 'practicing medicine' I guess." I roll over. I have the spins.

"Dr. Mason's office isn't picking up. Her cell number isn't working. The directory isn't working. No one is doing their job."

"Maybe she's on vacation?"

"They'd have someone in her place, interim," she sighed. "They can't just do this to their patients."

"Read the label, what does it say?"

"Uh," she scrunches her nose and squints her eyes at the orange bottle. "Oxycodine, ketamine, DCL-36, and then strings and strings of numbers and letters."

"Well, we got painkillers and… what's ketamine?"

Sara looks to the ceiling and thinks for a second. I see her deep in academic thought, tracing memories and education that she could wield so fiercely, but which so seldomly shows its face.

"Ketamine… is used before procedures. It's a painkiller, too, but more like an anesthetic."

"Look at you, Sherlock,"

"Listen, dick, we both took the same biology classes."

"Okay, but what's the other stuff. DCL-36 and all the gibberish?"

"No idea, Kev," her eyes dropped to the floor and she sat on the couch. "Hey, let's go clear our mind for a bit. Don't take anymore, we'll go get lunch or something then start trying to get into contact again with the doctor's office."

My stomach thought this was a good idea and I agreed.

I would not be happy with the findings.

CHAPTER TWENTY-FOUR

"Kevin," Sara begins. "What if… what if it has something to do with your drinking?"

Immediately I am resistant to the idea. My addiction has created a well-maintained resilience to the idea that I may be at error, but I mull it over for a few seconds. It makes sense. My personal timeline does not add up. How long have I been on this medication, a blend of painkillers and this bizarre DCL-36? How long have I been binging and taking these pills, leaving only a blue, powdery residue in the wake of my hangovers.

"I don't know, Sara. I mean, you might be right. But I've had issues long before this bullshit, right?"

She nods.

"Let's… I don't know," I begin. "Let's look around. Get customer reviews and that kind of thing."

Sara plants herself on the couch and begins typing away on her cellphone. I move over half-a-room and power up my computer. I go to my search engine of choice and begin searching various phrases involving the drugs on the label.

Substance abuse.

Painkillers.

Over the counters.

Prescription pain relievers.

I find absolutely nothing of value. I keep looking. Eventually, Jerry and Ted both text me, sending similar regards and messages about my well-being. I tell them what Sara and I are doing this afternoon and they promise to lend their productive efforts. I picture Jerry at Millie's house, entertaining her parents and I picture Ted fucking whatever girl he was seeing at the moment. Or his girlfriend. I do not remember what is actually the reality-based standard. But I appreciate their help.

After some more wandering around on the Internet, Sara comes back into the living room, pulling one of my sweatshirts over her head, looking for her car keys. I turn from my desk and peer through the entrance to my office. "Where are you going?" I ask.

"Do you want to go to Mason's? Just, straight up ask her about it, what she's been giving you?"

It was pragmatic and to the point, features severely lacking from the relationships I fostered. I loved it.

"Sure," I said. "Let me get my shoes."

The drive over is peaceful, yet meaningful. It is still raining, but there is always some precipitation in Deptford. I gently tap in time to the classic rock lightly playing over the radio and even though there is a look of irritated determination in Sara's eyes as she scans the road, busy driving, the atmosphere is nice. We are not arguing. We are working together. The feeling is smothered, soon enough. "Oh, what the fuck," Sara grits.

We pull into the office complex where the doctor had her practice. It was a rather normal American installation: a few dozen offices, some medical, some tax-based, some vacant and advertised as being open to lease. But it was not any of these, any longer. The handful of acres that made up this lot was razed. There was a lot of black dust, charred chunks of wood and stone, and some destroyed furniture. There was not any police tape, or caution signs, or anything signaling that this was, merely days ago, a highly-functioning facility. It was an act of an angry god, smiting Deptford for its rampant sodomy and tax-evasion, clearly.

"What the... what do you think happened?" I ask her. She puts the car into park and unbuckles her seatbelt. We both get out.

"I have no idea," she looks at the mess, her hands on her head.

"Maybe there was an electrical fire?" I offer.

"Maybe," she says. "But you would have thought it would have made the news or something."

"You don't think..." I stare past the lot and into the tree line beyond.

"...think what?" Sara prods me to continue. I reach into my pocket and remove my bottle of medicine.

"That it's like, some sort of insurance dodge on Mason's part, eh? What if she knew she was giving terrible medicine and it's finally caught up with her and—"

"I don't think so, Kevin. Missie – er, Dr. Mason – wouldn't do that. You were only one patient,"

"I suppose you're right," I rationalize. "But now what?" A thought hits me. "Fuck. Now this means I have to go see the hospital doctors for my rehab." I had forgotten how sweet of a deal it was, working with Agatha Mason.

"I just hope they're alright," Sara fiddles with her sleeve and stares at the debris.

"I fucking knew it!"

Sara looks over from the couch, from watching television, and her eyes read knew what?

"Jerry just texted me. He and Ted and found this bit of news about a drug recall affecting British Columbia, Washington, Idaho, Oregon, and... New Jersey, but that's not important. They think it's more widespread than that, but the bad drugs have been definitely traced there. Let me find the article..."

Sara walks over and we read the same material that my friends had notified me about. We both read the half-page or so of information and look at each other.

"Well," Sara said. "You definitely have some settlement money heading your way," she smiles, but then it fades. "But the article only mentions the oxycodone."

"And?"

"Meaning, we still don't know why you were taking an anesthetic and that mystery drug, 36, or whatever."

"You're right," I nod. "But I'm going to stop taking it either way."

"Good."

We sit on the couch, against one another, wrapped in blankets, and watch her favorite show. We end up sitting through a marathon, as we own the boxed-set collection, and I am enjoying our time together, bundled up. A gentle rain falls outside. When I stand to go to the bathroom, Jerry responds to the message I sent hours ago, updating our status. He's gone full Sherlock and tells me that he and Ted had found something, but Ted had to go home and get some sleep for work. They had been working all night, the clever little fucks. Jerry tells me that he took off the next few days of work and that I should take it easy and enjoy my night. We'll have "an adventure" tomorrow.

The Benjamin Macy Memorial Hospital had been closed for decades.

It sat atop a gentle range of sloping mountains and forests on the edge of Deptford County and was, at various points of his history, a tuberculosis refuge, a general hospital, and, most prominently, an asylum. Its decline came with the rise of other regional facilities and how inconvenient it was to drive up mountain roads for medical assistance.

It was not too far from my neighborhood and Jerry suggested we visit the old structure, so he could get me out of the house and catch me up on what they had discovered. After turning onto a dirt road, we got out of the car and walked about a mile into the woods, following a broken trail. There really was no need for this hands-on account of the property, but it was interesting to see my friends so enthusiastic about an actually pressing matter. The trail declined and opened up into a huge, open field. It was mottled with weeds and terribly overgrown, but on top of the hill sat the beast. A gigantic stone face, lined with ivy, growth, and decay, stared at us in the grey afternoon light. It was three stories tall and its wings tore off into multiple-volumes in either direction. All of its windows were open, lacking any glass or protection, and its main entrance was easily accessible. We walked up the hill and sat on the large concrete steps. Jerry fiddled with his smartphone and brought up his notes before speaking.

"Okay, so you know how Ted loves all those ghost-hunting shows and the History Channel and all that?"

I nod, peeking into the dark building and its contrast against the open field. I wish I had brought my camera.

"Well, when he was younger, he always loved going into these places and looking for scary stories, all of that stuff,"

"Yeah, he made a website in high school dedicated to 'urban exploring' – he took nice pictures, and I always thought he was always going to get raped by a homeless person or something."

"Yes," Jerry scrolled down his phone. "He extensively studied these old buildings and their histories whenever he would visit them and then write about them on his site. When you told us about 'DCL-36', neither of us had any firsthand knowledge about the drugs, but Ted said he felt like he had read about it somewhere, and he started goofing around through his old writing."

"Alright," I said. I stand up and feel the smooth coldness of the walls and walk around in the foyer. I can see where the reception desk once functioned. On either side of me, halls run in either direction and stairwells allow for access to the higher floors. Through the arches, you can see the hallways running straight, either way, for what feels like eternity.

At the far end, for just a moment, I see an old man in an olive military uniform. Even at a hundred yards, I can see him wink, smile, salute, and then turn on heel. But when I blink he's gone. Turning around offers me no solace: I see the young couple from the night we got ice cream, walking away. Young me in a large jacket, holding a young Mariah's hand. She's dressed in white. She drops a freshly-picked sunflower and, of course, they are gone with a series of blinks. I rub my eyes and try to concentrate on Jerry's story.

"Well, whatever drug it actually is, it was manufactured here in Deptford County in the forties! It was born here."

"That's... interesting."

Jerry stands and enters the building to speak directly to me. He is excited and it bothers me a little bit.

"Kevin, actually here. At Benjamin Macy Memorial. There was an on-site lab somewhere and they had actually tested it on patients, back in the crazy days of medicine."

"Oh, shit," I nod. "Maybe that's why they eventually closed, or went out of business. Whatever."

"Yes," Jerry looked at his phone. "So Ted was looking at his old site and all of the correspondence and comments it picked up from the net and he saw an old message from an enthusiast that collected antique pieces and records about hospitals. And he claimed to be an 'expert' on Benjamin Macy Memorial."

I walk towards the left side and stand at the threshold of the hall. Jerry continues.

"Ted had emailed the guy, years ago, and they were decent online friends. The kid moved from Deptford when he was in middle school, but you guys probably would have known him if he stayed around. He now lives in Seattle."

I didn't really want to go to Seattle, especially just to find out why my doctor was a piss-poor medical practitioner.

"Jerry, listen," I turned and put my hand on his shoulder. "I appreciate all of this, and it's amazing just how small of a world it is, with what Ted remembers and whatnot. But I'm fine. I'll wait for the class action lawsuit to arise, I'll get my sum of money, and we'll forget about this."

For once in the duration that I knew and considered Jerry a friend, he did not take my words as those of wisdom. For once, the thoughts pouring from his mind to his mouth were his own. They were thoughts of conspiracy, of something greater than he, of something beyond the walls of his office, beyond the realm of his nine-to-five / find a wife / don't kill yourself / and enjoy your prime time television routine.

"Kevin, you don't think… life has been a bit strange, recently?"

I laughed.

"A fucking loaded statement, don't you think, Jerry?"

"No, I mean… yeah, you've always had a temper. And maybe our office wasn't really fit to your style. But, just think, it's all been a… spiral since you quit. And it's not the Swedish guy's fault. It's not bad luck. It's just… a lot. You go into a coma for a month, something fucks with your air conditioner, you, who had been comfortably employed since college, can't hold a job for more than a week after a freak out… it's just. I don't know. Maybe I watch too many movies."

I wanted to correct him and say, "two month coma," but he had just poured his soul out. There was a metric ton of conviction in his reasoning. I did not know how to really respond, but I felt the sincerity in his plea to listen to his words. So, I nodded, and turned to pace.

"Yeah, fine," I said. "Tell Ted to let this dude know we'll drive up and meet him. Purely business though, this ain't going to be some reunion love-fest."

"Awesome," Jerry said. "Ted probably won't even want to go though, so don't worry about that. I'll call him, we can take some pictures, and then we'll head out, alright?"

Jerry waved his phone throughout this agenda, pantomiming a camera with his cellphone in hand, and then turned and started dialing Ted. I leaned in the archway of the hall and stared down the dizzying depth.
It was one of those illusions, a hall of open doors and open floor-space, all painted and decaying at the same rate. It may have even been more intoxicating during its functioning years. It would all be painted the same dull colors and lit with the same artificial lighting. For a second, I can picture it perfectly. Jerry's voice echoes from the front entrance and I walk a few paces into the hall. I crouch down and pick up a single sunflower left forgotten on the floor.

CHAPTER TWENTY-FIVE

I could not remember if I had ever visited Seattle as an adult.

I may have as a child, but I certainly had not been here within the last decade of my life. Jerry was like a pig in shit. The typical road trip banter informed me that he had been here once with his parents when he a kid. He told me loved it, that he swore he had a picture of him at the "first Starbucks," that they saw all the sights, and all that useless nonsense. The drive was only a few hours and I slept for the bulk of it. Jerry listened to some acoustic, mildly pretentious music and I swore to myself that he would fit right in.

Ted had wanted to come, to actually meet up with this old friend from the Internet from so many years before, but I guess he had already used too much of his personal time at work. Jerry just didn't care, or his elephant-like immune system granted him the luxury of calling out. Or maybe I just liked calling him an elephant. Every so often, he'd get a call or a text message from Millie checking in. It was cute the first half-a-dozen times, but then I started harboring distaste for their relationship. Hopefully the newness of it all would wear thin soon.

I was awake and alert for the last hour of the ride, taking in the scenery and rapidly civilizing landscape.

"So what's this guy's name?"

"Uh, it's Allen Frinkman," Jerry said, glancing at his GPS on the console.

"Allen Frinkman," I snorted.

I took out my phone and typed his name in on the Internet browser. Within seconds, I found this guy's personal site and a bunch of contact information.

"He goes by Frink?" I deadpanned.

"Hey, listen," Jerry said, raising a hand. "Ted vouched for his guy."

I read some more on his site.

"Jerry, Frink owns a head shop and describes himself as a 'connoisseur of lighting up' – he's not a historian, he collects antiques… antiques about smoking. Oh, god damn it."

"Dude, it'll be fine."

"We're not going to his shop, right?"

"No, no, Ted got his home address. His grandfather lives with him."

"You mean, he lives with his grandfather."

"Nah, it sounded like he takes care of him, like the old dude's disabled or something."

"Fucking great," my head fell against the window. "We get to talk to Cheech Jr. while a dribbling mannequin stares at us from the corner."

"Chill, man," Jerry said, looking at me. "He'll help us out. Figure out what this bullshit is." He pointed at the bottle of medicine in the cup holder.

      The house was beautiful and rather old. It was at the far end of town, where houses actually had yards and were not strung together in a row. It was painted light brown and had chocolate trimming everywhere else. "Frink" was waiting for us on the ornate front steps when we pulled up. "Gentlemen!" he shook our hands.

He was skinny and looked young. His skin was pale and he had deep bags under his eyes. One of his ears bore one of those insufferable quarter-sized gauges and he had his eyebrow pierced. His head was shaved and he wore a hooded-sweatshirt that was too big and black jeans that were too skinny. He correctly guessed who was who (between Jerry and I) and then brought us inside.

We sat in the living room and he gave us cans of Coke. Jerry immediately opened his and sat with his planted on his knee. I thanked Frink for the soda and left it unopened on the floor. His grandfather, whom he introduced as Ben, sat in a wheelchair in the corner (as predicted) and watched the news on TV. After making eye contact with us and twitching his arm in greeting, he faced slightly away from us and stared at the box with moving pictures. He wore a plastic strip plugged into his nose and kept an oxygen tank at his feet. Without these accessories, he would look like a healthy old man. As he was, however, he was decrepit.

Frink excitedly leaves the room and returns with a stack of papers in a plastic binder. He tells me that he loved what Ted did when they were growing up and wrote similar articles. However, he did not have a computer until he was college-aged, so most of them just became childhood relics kept in this binder. There was a piece of masking tape across its cover that bore the words DEPTFORD COUNTY: HISTORY in permanent marker. He explained that as he grew up and matured, his love for Deptford's history remained, so he kept the binder and always added to it. He kept speaking, but flipped through the pages as he did so, looking for something. He finally stopped on a page featuring newspaper clippings and text and looked up. "Alright, so you guys said it was 'DCL-36' – correct?"

"Yes," I said.

"Well," he momentarily tugged at his ear piercing. "That was probably one of the last batches made up at the hospital," he turned to Jerry. "I heard that you showed the property to Kevin?" He gestured towards me and smiled.

"Yeah, we took a drive up there,"

"Oh yeah? How's it holding up?"

"Ah," Jerry said. "Decently, I guess. It was just very overgrown. Right, Kevin?"

"Sure."

"Right, well," Frink looked back at the book. "Moving on."

"What did you mean, 'batches'?" Jerry asked.

"Oh, right," Frink explained. "Well, there were many, many tests done on the patients up there. You know how it was: if you were retarded or something, they just screwed with you. Your families didn't really care. Some of these tests included in-house concoctions of medicines. I'm using the word 'medicine' loosely – it was just mixtures of chemicals, really. Almost like what the Nazis did during the war, but with less expected deaths."

He looked up at us. Jerry was really interested, but I just wanted to know what he was getting at.

"The medicines were created in series, that's why I said 'batch,' but they all did different things as they were testing different ideas and abuses on the patients. Series 1-5 were really humane. It was basically testing pot and its effect on the demeanor of the patients. It was coded DCL-1, DCL-2, etc., or 'Deptford County Lab, Series 1' and on and on and on. It gave no real chemical indication on what the substance was. Specific production numbers were sometimes printed after, too."

"So, what was DCL-36?" I asked.

"Like I was saying before, it was one of the last ones tested before they closed," he ran his finger through lines of text and turned the page. "Ah, yup. Actually the last one. Series 36 – 40 were supposed to involve meditation and amnesia, but they only had one active test, batch thirty-six, because the hospital was then closed. Apparently, a few of the subjects died of arsenic-like poisoning."

"Wonderful," I blinked.

"Oh, you have nothing to worry about, I am sure whatever you took was diluted. No way could that fly these days. I'm just unsure how they got national… like, authorization to manufacture it—"

"I don't think they did." I grit.

"Oh?"

"No," I stood. "The only reason I'm here is because I've been taking this bullshit and having incredible migraines and lapses in the hours of my waking life. I am terrified because this rubbish has, apparently, only ever surfaced once before, and that was at some weird torture hospital in the mountains, a hundred years ago!"

"Calm down, Kev," Jerry stood and touched my shoulder. We sat.

"Oh," Frink said, looking up. "I didn't realize the extent. I assumed you found a bottle of it or something in storage."

"No, I guess we didn't do a sufficient job at explaining why this meeting was so urgent."

"Well… I'm willing to at least make it a little worthwhile for you. I don't know if you knew this, but I collect—"

"Yes, I saw your website."

"Oh, cool. Well, yeah, I collect medical antiques and I actually have samples of many of the DCL productions. Just not thirty-six. Would you mind…" he turned around and dug in his pocket.

"What, like, selling it to you?" I took out the bottle and shook it. "Dude, you can take some. I don't fucking want it. I just need to keep a little for whenever this lawsuit comes about."

"Oh, excellent," he rose and put the book down. "Let me go get a vial or something."

As he left, Jerry looked over at me.

"Well, at least he knows what he's talking about. We'll go get dinner or something, check in at the hotel, and then we'll have him gather anything he can about those studies and make copies for us before we leave tomorrow morning."

"Sure."

He came back into the room wearing rubber gloves and an open vial that you would buy at a craft store. He also held a corked sample of another substance, a light pink powder.

"Those of us in the hobby, us collectors," he explained, handing me the bottle of pink powder. "Don't really like being gifted special pieces without just compensation. I told you, I have some of the whole DCL set, but not 36. You're holding what I believe, well, at least what was labeled as 34."

"What did the 31-35 batch set out to accomplish?" I asked.

"Oh, I don't know. It was a prelude to the whole meditation study in the upper thirties that never came about. Something about consciousness and focus. Sounds like cocaine if you ask me."

"Listen, man, I don't really need to 'trade' with you—" I gently pushed his hand away.

"No, I insist," he placed the vial in my palm. "It's only fair. Just don't use it!" he laughed.

"Is... is this hobby... legal?" Jerry asked.

"Oh, not at all," Frink smirked. "We're basically time-travelling drug dealers."

"Oh," shared Jerry and I.

"Well, can you show me what you were taking?"

I put the vial Frink gave me into my pocket and began unscrewing the orange bottle holding the blue pills. I guess shaking them up broke a few, but there was still a good amount left. I put the cap down and handed the bottle to Frink. He peered into them and then shifted towards the light, which was emitted from a lamp near grandpa in the corner.

"Fascinating..." he gently tilted the bottle towards his open palm and shook out a few pills.

One, two, three drop into his hand in a miniature avalanche of the blue dust. I realize that his grandfather has been facing us for some time now. As this dust settles, catching the off-beam of light from the lamp, the old man begins fussing in his chair. He bends over, struggling, the wheels locked but rocking back and forth against his weight, and he drags the oxygen tank in front of him and moves to stand up. A great deal of wheezing and struggled breathing comes from the plastic in his nose and from his mouth.

"Grandpa?" Frink closes his hands on the pills and hands me the bottle. "Pop, what's wrong?"

Struggling to his feet and shaking violently, the old man lugs his oxygen up to waist-level so he can walk.

"Get… get…" he is shaking a finger directly at me and Jerry. "Get those fools out of my house. Get them out of my house!"

Frink bottles the pills and caps it, rapidly placing it into his pocket and then tears off his gloves and moves to help his grandfather.

"Pop, you're going to fall again," he pleads. "Calm down, calm down, they're just collectors like me. Like my pipes and stuff? You know them! You like looking at the metal ones. Sit down, grandpa, please!"

Jerry and I glance at one another, not sure if we should help or evade the oncoming assault of the geriatric. Frink grabs the oxygen tank from the man's weak grasp and with his other hand pushes him back towards the chair. With a terrible popping and snapping sound, the old man tears his breathing apparatus out of his nostrils and off of his head and ambles towards us. Jerry raises his hands, distancing himself from confrontation as the man tackles me onto the hardwood. He is breathing like a rabid dog and smells of applesauce and shoe polish.

He would be attempting to straddle me and to punch my face, but he is far too weak, so instead, he simply tackles me and is shouting nonsense.

"Allen, they're Banner's boys, Allen. Get them away from here. They'll only bring trouble. They're Banner's boys, damnit!"

Eventually, Frink rolls him off of me and into his chair. He drops the oxygen tank into his lap and apologizes. He urges us to leave and promises he'll get in touch later. He wheels the man away as Jerry and I stare after them, wide-eyed.

We are driving for about ten minutes, towards the hotel. We have been silent, not sharing a single thought. Then, we both start laughing. Hysterically.

"What the hell just happened?" he says behind laughing tears.

"I have no fucking clue, man," I say. "Ted knows how to pick them, huh?"

We get to the hotel and Jerry is beat-tired. He apologizes that he's not more lively, but he was, also, the one driving all day. I say it's fine, I'm just going to go look for somewhere to get food that's still open.

The night is a little chilly, but for once it's not raining. I end up stopping in a coffee shop of all places, getting a sandwich and sitting at a little counter, facing the glass window on the sidewalk. It's nothing special and no one bothers me. I am content. Upon leaving, I see a storefront that is closed, since it is approaching midnight. It is obviously a tourist attraction. It promotes the "Seattle Underground!" and has ticket listings and tour times. I put my hand against the door and think for a second. No way in hell would it be – I push and the door is open. Ha.

I walk through the small store space and see a velvet rope halting entrance down a flight of stairs. I assume that this is where the tour would queue during the day. I take out my phone and enable a flashlight setting, making sure that no one saw me enter from the street and I make sure that the door is now actually closed. I remove the velvet rope from its latch.

It is incredible. Dusty, yes, and hell on my allergies, but very rarely will anything ever be as simple of a sublimity as this. I walk down the stairs and through the gangway of what appears to be a construction site to find myself on an underground boardwalk. During operating hours, lamps would guide my way, but I do not know where the switches are. I am walking the streets of Seattle, decades in the past. At a certain point in time, the city planners must have decided that battling the sea level and potential flood waters was not worth the risk and literally built over their existing street.

I find old wooden storefronts, delis, restaurants, housing, and even a bank. Calling to me from the past, I manage to find a bar. I step over the handrail and touch the door. The old, faded piece feels strangely warm to my touch and I force my way in. I did not expect there to even be an open space. I assumed they filled in the old levels of these buildings, but perhaps some of the existing properties upstairs, on street level, use these as basements. The parlor area of the bar is spacious. There is a hall to the back, but it appears to be filled in with brick. I sit down on a random chair in the center of the room and sit back, quietly smiling at the serenity of my being and the peculiarity of my location. The door I eased open closes without my influence and I am torn from my zen-state.

I shoot the light towards the door and find nothing. No ghosts underground, Kevin. They were all washed away. I crack myself up. But in the tunnel vision of my entrance, I failed to notice something on the wall. When I panicked and scanned the room, I realized that I had walked right past some wonderful graffiti. I approached the faded blue chipping wall of the bar and feel its coolness. What appears to be a simple, but masterfully done, depiction of Lenny, the manatee-elephant-monster-god from back home, is painted onto the wall. It looks like it was done with charcoal. At his shoulder, a crude human figure wearing a crown is also drawn, with a mustard colored robe faded as its length wears on.

I think, Sal would get a kick out of this, and quickly take a picture of it, utilizing my phone's camera. Huh. Who would have considered: finding Deptford's influence underground, halfway across the state. I send the picture to Mitch, hoping that he will see Sal before I do. I highly doubted that Sal had a phone capable of receiving pictures, so that was my no-thought-process-needed wager. Glancing back at the art on the wall, I get the chills and the odd sensation that I am in a room full of strangers. I quickly turn around, sweeping it with my light, and I am, of course, alone.

Looking the art one more time, my breath catches. Perhaps it is the charcoal lines, perhaps it is the macabre nature of it all, perhaps I am breathing asbestos in and that is the culprit, but I am brought to a momentary state of syncope and nausea as I remember a dream I had a few weeks ago. I remember straddling the girl, I remember the paint, I remember murdering an innocent girl in my dreams and I choke the memory away, gasping for air. You need help, Kevin. You need some gentle psychiatric help.

I leave the empty bar, close the door behind me, and search for the boardwalk. I find no such purchase upon my feet. It is day time. This old street does belong to Seattle, but does not belong to the era from which I stepped down into. I am on a busy street in Deptford and people are rushing past me, excited, happy, shouting. I see a large crowd of people at the far end, gathering around a small stage. I start walking towards it in a gaze. Organic sunlight warms my skin.

"People of Deptford," I hear a voice booming. "I am pleased to announce—"

My head explodes in pain with each staccato burst of speech.

"—the grand opening of—"

Searing pain, flames, thunder, radiation.

"—Bannersville!"

The crowd erupts into cheering and I am brought to my knees in painful agony. I look up towards the bright spring sky and blink. The sun is blinding and I cannot rid myself of the pure blindness.

"Hey, who the hell's down here?"

I blink and the intensity of the light dies. My eyes were not prepared for the string of lamps to turn on, down here in the dark. I am back in Seattle, underground. A voice is calling towards me, the intruder from around a corner. I duck into an alley and crouch. An older man holding a crowbar walks past. Obviously the owner or someone employed by the touring company. Across the street from my hiding spot, I see the old storefront of an clockmaker. It's sign reads, "Hello, friend. It is time!"

"The door was unlocked and the rope is down. Don't make me call the cops!"

As he rounds the corner, I hold my breath and shuffle towards the entrance, keeping off of the noisy boardwalk and keeping my petrified sprints on the loose sandy soil. When I hit the stairs running, he immediately hears my footsteps and shouts in my direction, but I am already gone, absorbed into the city streets, two blocks away, before he could even hope to catch me.

CHAPTER TWENTY-SIX
I get back to the hotel and Jerry is fast asleep.

I don't disturb him. I find my bag and get undressed and into comfortable clothes for sleep. I lay my phone on the end table and go into the bathroom to do my nightly routine. I hear a dull vibration on the wood, indicating that someone somewhere out there wishes to bother me with a text message.

I am not a particularly anxious person. You know this. I do not find hesitation and fear in the most mundane of human activities and the greater impact of social interactions. I simply do not like to partake in them. However, upon hearing that vibration, with the toothbrush in my mouth, I feel an immense and immediate pang of fear. Like Christ and the last supper, I rinse my mouth of the toothpaste and turn out the bathroom light, walking towards the end table. The body and blood of Christ, Crest Ultra and a hotel's tap water. I sit on my bed and look at my phone. It is a message from Mitch. It reads: Have you seen Sal?

I tell him no. He tells me he cannot get a hold of him.
I call Sal. No one picks up.
I call Sal again. No one picks up.
I call him once more and the line is dead.

I am not one to panic, but the bluntness in Mitch's messages frightens me. Mitch would always take the edge off. I think of my grandmother. I think of her and Sal and Margaret and how they were the most important elderly people in my life. My mind paints terrible scenarios: maybe Margaret had a stroke and Sal had to rush her to the hospital. Maybe Sal fell and Margaret was too inept to help him. I think of my grandmother. How did she die? Heart disease, or was it cancer? Why wasn't I smart to enough to help her? Why wasn't I there with her? I think of my grandfather. Did she help him when he died? How did he die? What was it like for my grandmother to die alone?

I am physically ill from this hydra-head of poor possibilities, branching off into a dozen different pessimistic tendrils of ill-thought and death. Somehow, I find sleep.

Not two hours later I am awake, my phone blinking a notification light on its side indicating that I've missed calls. One from Sara, two from Mitch, and none from Sal. I also have one text message from Mitch. It simply says: Sal's apartment complex is on fire. He wasn't inside. Still no word from him.

I am wide awake.

CHAPTER TWENTY-SEVEN

"Jerry, wake the fuck up!"

I beat him in the face with a pillow multiple times. I discard the pillow and shake him from the shoulders. He opens his eyes, bloodshot and unrested, and looks around the room, and then up at me.
"What the hell, man?"
"We have to go back," I am sweeping around the room, picking up my few clothes and grabbing my toiletries from the bathroom.
"Go where? Home?"
"Yes. Now. Please."
"But what about Frink? He wanted to meet—"

"Fuck Frink, man," my life is stricken with terrible alliterations, puns, and word associations. "Something's going on."
Jerry sits up.
"What do you mean, Kevin?" he is solemn, curious, and sincere.
I stop my mad dash around the hotel room.

"Listen, I don't know what's happening. But… everything you said before. I don't know. I'm anxious. I'm feeling like I'm on the cusp of a panic attack and it just won't crest. It feels like… like everything's coming to a head. I don't know. Sal's apartment building is on fire—"
"Whoa, whoa, whoa, is he okay? What about that lady he lives with?"
"Yes, well, no. I don't know. He's missing, dude. Mitch says he can't get in touch with him. Sara tried calling me… wait. Listen. You try and get into touch with Ted. Tell him to let himself in at my house and stay the night. If we have a refugee-level Sal needing a place to stay, I want someone there to let him. I'm going to try to call Sara back and see what the fuck's going on. I'm sure Mitch has talked to her."

And there, like two schmucks trying to plug a leaking dam with their fingers, we paced the room, listening to cell phones silent sans ominous, monotonous ringing. We each stand there for ten minutes, redialing and hoping to hear a living voice and no one picks up.
"Let me get my things," Jerry gets changed and gathers his belongings. His hair is messy and many dead curls fall over his face.

We are checked out of the hotel and on the road within fifteen minutes. The clerk asked if we wanted a refund, or if anything was wrong with the room, and I promised that there was nothing wrong with the room and that the free sample of soap in the bathroom which smelled of vanilla was wonderful.

We speed past Frink's house and not a single light is on.

I am, of course, continuously redialing the list of our friends. Borderline psychotic? Maybe. Annoying? Absolutely. Futile? As of yet, that too.

I do this for the duration of the ride home.

CHAPTER TWENTY-EIGHT
The hours are unbearable.

I am leaning forward, staring into the dark road, mechanically redialing my list of contacts. No one is answering. Jerry's stomach growls and he says nothing. I wonder what the man in the underground is doing now, if he gave up his search for intruders or if he's still fruitlessly poking around in the dust. Maybe he thinks it was a ghost, that my stomping feet were just whispers of the past. Maybe he'll use it as a marketing ploy and earn some money from the paranormal-loving demographics.

I think of the odd mental episode I had in the street, of the crowd of people in a place called Bannersville. This, of course, makes me think about old man Frinkman and his grandson. Why did we offend that decrepit old fuck so terribly? Why was it that he freaked out and had unnatural strength upon seeing the blue powder? What were they doing now? And why did he associate me with Joseph Banner?

We are about twenty minutes from home when Jerry takes the penultimate exit. We would take this highway, drive fifteen minutes, exit, and be nearly there. But as we prepare to enter the last stretch of road, we are affronted with the burden of choice. The highway divides into two four-lane portions: CARS and CARS, TRUCKS, AND BUSES. Both entrances have CLOSED signs in front of them and no sign of construction vehicles or police enforcers.
"What are we supposed to..." I question aloud.

"Well, whenever a road is closed, it's always marked 'open to local traffic' – I guess…" he inches the car forward and merges onto the highway.

"If we see land movers and lights and shit then we turn off. Last thing we need are cops and tickets and bullshit and…" I mumble to myself, anxious to get home and find everyone, safe.

We pass under the red blinking lights affixed to the CLOSED sign and cruise down the ramp and onto the interstate. There is not a single light or car for miles in either direction. We both stop at the merge lane and look either way. There's no one coming from the opposite side. Our decision is made for us.

"Well, fuck it," I shrug and Jerry speeds up to the normal pace.

I need a distraction. I turn on the car's radio and flick the option to CD. Jerry has the album OK Computer loaded in and the second track begins playing. I stare forward and tap the drum and bass section on the window.

"Jerry!" I put my hand out against his chest to brace for an impact, even though he is the one driving.

We screech to a halt.

"Dude," Jerry mutters, putting the car into park. We both look at each other and then what is in the middle of the road. We get out.

There, in the middle of the highway, is a waist-height carving of the folklore god Lenny. It is masterfully crafted and carved of a deeply shaded marble. The thing must weigh a ton. It is just Jerry and I standing side by side, staring at this carving. Easily could have destroyed the front of his car If we were to strike it at sixty-or-so miles per hour. We would have broken a few bones each and not died, but still. Close call.

"Who do you think moved it out here?" he asks.

"No idea, man," I put my hand on it.

It is cool against my skin, but leaves an odd tingling sensation. The car's headlights behind us is our only source of light on this Pacific highway. There is the light, our shadows, and the statue. Then, the headlights vanish and there is only darkness.

I turn towards Jerry and hear his breathing catch. We both turn back towards the car, but I hear a heavy, wet, thud and am lacking a Jerry-sized silhouette on my right. I look around, hear the same sound, this time amplified 120% and accompanied by a searing pain on the back of my head. We have both be beaten down by blunt objects. Consciousness fades and I feel blood on my neck.

My eyes open and I feel the weight of the ocean on my skull. I am in the back of a police cruiser.
My hands are bound behind my back with duct tape, as is my mouth. My ankles are tied together and I am all too aware of the wound on my head. The cruiser's lights are on. There are lots of people outside. They are all wearing black. Black business suits, or black robes, it is all a mix. I see two figures on their knees, also bound, near the statue. It is Jerry and Sal. Sal has a bag over his head, but I would recognize that man a mile away. His navy blue jacket with the golden buttons betrays him. Jerry does too, but I was with him just moments ago. I know my friend. They are prisoners.

There is a low murmur of chanting. They are too far, too deep, and too low for me to understand any of it. A tall figure steps out in front. As with my friends, I can recognize this man, even through his disguise: it is the pharmacist, Art, in a black suit, black shirt, black tie, and black mesh covering his head. Over this, he wears a small, black, metallic theatre mask. The one he wore to masquerade. The wine tasting.

He wields a large blunt weapon, as well. I cannot discern the symbols on it from this distance, but it is something you may find in a museum, a religious piece belonging to an old civilization. It is essentially, a stone club, with contemporary accents, such as metal plating at portions, engraved in a tongue I cannot read. Art shouts something and the mob of people yell in precise response. One of them removes Jerry's hood and pushes him against the statue, his neck exposed to the sky, his head, on top of the deity. Art raises the club and I start shrieking, muffled behind the gag. I realize that a member of this procession has been standing outside of the car this whole time. Upon my screaming, he opens the door and removes the orange bottle of pills that was mine, hours ago. He crushes the blue pills in his hand, leans into the car, and holds me by the back of my head. The pain is immediate and the interaction with my bloodstream is just as reactive.

The drug is back in me at an insane dosage and I find it hard to keep my eyes open. The guard rubs it into my open wound and leaves the car, closing the door behind me. I slouch forward. I watch the group of people expose their palms to the heavens and then clench their hands into fists. Art aims the club at Jerry's head and I see the terror in my friend's eyes. There is no way that he can see me from this distance, but he stares directly at me, through the windshield. Art brings the club down in a sweeping arc and I blink.

When I hope my eyes, minutes have passed, surely an act of the drug. Jerry's body lies, dead, discarded, closer to the car and away from the crowd. They are finished with him. Sal is now kneeling before Art, but not yet on the slab. They remove Sal's hood and the murmuring chant begins again.

Art says something to Sal and Sal looks up at the crowd and then at Art. Then he looks past them, at me, back in the car. I obviously cannot hear him, but I know he is talking about me. The chanting is brought to an even less audible level and Art turns and walks towards the car. He whispers something to my guard near my window and they both look at me. Art returns to his altar and the guard opens the car door, cutting my ankle-binds with a box cutter. Surprisingly gentle and without a word, he takes me from the car and walks me over to the ceremony. I make sure to stand in front of Sal, so he is not burdened by the brilliance of the car's spotlight. He smiles upon squinting his eyes through broken glasses and focusing on me.

"I'm sure this is all a bit strange for you," he admits.
The syncope of standing near my dead friend strikes me and I want to vomit. I want to cry. I want to be home.
"W-what's... what's happening, Mr. Delange?"
At the mention of his name, he chuckles.
"Oh, you know to call me 'Sal' at this point, dearest Kevin,"
The chanting continues around us, but otherwise, no one is speaking in conversation. Not even Art. Art stands, facing away from us, still, silent, waiting.
"Who... are these people?"
"They're our friends, Kevin,"
"Why, why did they kill Jerry?"
"Oh," he sighed. "The same reason they're getting rid of me."

I moved to help him, to release him, to punch any of these psychos, and escape with him, but at the slightest movement, the guard holds me by my wrists and reminds me that I was still bound in such a manner. My head throbs and I lose vision in my left eye.
"Don't worry, Kevin. Everything will be explained soon enough. Please, do enjoy the Fair without me—" the person behind Sal delivers a swift kick to his back and Sal loses his breath. He spits, stumbling over, and straightens himself out.

197

"What a touchy bunch. I love you all," he smiles and looks around the group.

Sal looks at all of them with a smile. Every. Last. One. He looks at Art, whose back is turned, and clears his throat.

"Oh, Arty," Sal sing-songs. "I'm ready for my close-up."

I again move to intervene and am halted in place by the guard.

"Sal..."

He looks into my eyes, smiles, and a single tear runs down his cheek.

"Kevin," he sniffs. "If we had another hour together, I would explain everything. But we have no such comfort. You are all very, very busy tonight. Sixteen hours left, is that right, Andrew?" he looks towards the guard. The guard (named Andrew, apparently) makes no sound, no movement.

Sal shakes off his glasses and they land at my feet with a slight crackle of the frames.

"Slip those into Kevin's pocket, would you, Andrew?"

The guard looks at Art for confirmation and he nods, allowing it. The guard walks over, crouches, and retrieves the glasses. He lets them fall into my front pocket.

Between Sal on his knees and Jerry on his side and the blindness in my left eye, I cannot help but begin to cry. I cannot think straight, I cannot stand. I stumble and fall on my ass, my wrists still bound behind my back. Sal shuffles over to the marble statue on his knees, smirking.

"Fear not for me, Kevin," he promises. "I'll see you again. I've paid my share. We'll laugh about this. These fools... it's always the younger generation who thinks theirs is the last!" The old man has lost it. He is laughing. Art raises his club.

"Why was I in such a position of power and honor! I was always meant for the stage, dearies. I was merely a player!"

Art executes Salvatore Delange.

CHAPTER TWENTY-NINE

I am awake, but my eyes are closed.

No alarm assaults me. There is no warm body belonging to Sara next to me. I am not dreaming. I am awake and remotely aware of a distant throbbing in my head; not pain, no, just a simple awareness of alteration. Still in the world of darkness, under blankets, I raise my hand to my head and feel a recently showered head of hair. I feel a bump and the tender tissue of abuse, but I am not on the highway. I am not in the back of a car. I am not bleeding.

I bolt awake and am sitting in my bed, at home, alone. The clock says two pm. The stack of nurses' notes and health charts still sits on my end table. I feel like I did after I woke up from my two-month coma. I reach over and expect my bottle of medicine to be waiting for me. I remember that it was basically poison and causing me to lose time and memories. I also remember that some fucker in a black suit is carrying it. What happened? Was it all a dream? Was this all a bad dream? Was Sara about to come in and tell me that the guys were coming over for a party this weekend? Fuck. Jerry?

I stand and run to the bathroom. I wash my face off in the sink and stare at myself in the mirror. The bags under my eyes and the distant pain on my skull let me know that the past was real. Jerry was dead. He was dead because he was with me. I back into the wall and fall to the floor, breathing. There is one object on my person, in my pocket. Someone bathed me and changed me into my pajamas, but made sure that I had this in my possession: DCL-34.

"Kevin?"

I start and glance up.

"Mitch?"

Mitch is standing my bathroom doorway. He looks tired. He's in a dirty hoodie and jeans. He leans down and lifts me up. He leads me to the living room and sits down on the couch next to me. He has his hand on my shoulder.

"What... what day is it?" I ask him.

"You didn't miss any time. That was last night. I was there. I'm sorry."

"You were… you were with that… fucking crazy group—"

"Kevin, listen," he inhaled. "You know Deptford's a small place. The Conservation Society, they're… we're a close-knit group. They're not evil—"

"They murdered two people close me. They're not evil? What the fuck, Mitch—"

"Kev, please," he looked like he was on the verge of tears. "Just bear with me. Tonight is the commencement of the County Fair, just come with us and we'll—"

"The. Mother-fucking. County. Fair. Are you jacking me, Mitch? The fucking Fair – who gives a flying fuck about the county fair? People are dead—"

He slaps me.

"Kevin, do you want it straight?"

"…Okay?"

"You're not going to walk away, touting 'bullshit'?"

"…No promises."

"There's a cycle in play. You would not directly know of it, but you do have extensive knowledge of it, locked up. We've had you on medicine forever, even before your accident. You're… an asshole, Kevin. You're too arrogant, free-thinking, and complacent to help us naturally. So the Elders have been having you drugged for years. High school therapy, your college psychiatrist, all of them. Your college doctor was a bit harder to swap out… that's exactly why you were a pain in the ass. You were never supposed to leave Deptford. That's a large component of why you were fired from your job.

"You still lived here, but you were always at risk of leaving for the big time. You're an excellent programmer, man. And we all know this. But you have… royal blood."

"Royal blood? Get the fuck out. My grandmother died of heart disease years ago and my parents are alcoholics—"

"Kevin, your grandmother died according to the plan. Your parents aren't who you think they are, either. They're gone. Your real parents are somewhere across the world. They were paid off. They don't care. They're content. Don't ask why, but the cycle skips a generation. Your mother was murdered... well, sacrificed. Her time was up. She fucked Joseph Banner. He chose her. She knew what her role was."

"Joe Banner... what the fuck does he have to do with this?"

"Mr. Banner was your grandfather, Kevin. He did everything that Sal told you he did, through his stories. He tapped into something otherworldly when he was travelling the world. When he was comingling with the witchdoctors on the African continent or fucking eating children in Europe. He was out there, harnessing some wicked dark energy. And he brought it back here. Joseph Banner's your grandfather, Kevin. And he lives at the assisted living home on the coast. The castle."

I stood at the sink and poured myself a glass of water. My hands were shaking. I stared into the woods. There was no nature hike occurring today. It was drizzling outside.

Mitch stood in the kitchen and waited for me to say something. I offered him no conversation. I moved to my computer and half-heartedly checked my email and my sites. I had no interest in facing the bizarre verbal-diarrhea that Mitch was attempting to feed me. He was still waiting for me to engage him. I offered no entrance to my psyche until I finally stood up from my desk and moved back in the living room and collapsed to the floor, my hands covering my eyes.

"What... do you mean it's a cycle?"

Without missing a beat, Mitch continued.

"Banner brought a deity back to protect Deptford. Simultaneously, it required a blood compensation. We keep good health and separation from a super-developed society, and remain tucked away in the mountains in return for a few sacrificed lovers every few decades."

"I don't buy it."

"Kevin, that guy from the pharmacy?"

"What about him?"

"Art's 67 years old."

The fucker looked like he was thirty, maybe.

"So you're telling me that Banner killed his girlfriend years ago... and then my grandma? That's two people."

"I don't remember the ceremonial language used. It's something about 'the one they love and the one they kept' – it works itself out, Kevin. You cannot choose it."

I stood up and confronted Mitch.

"Okay," I grit, staring him in the eyes. "Then where are my two dead broads, huh? Where are my two dead lovers, huh?"

Mitch's eye twitched and then he looked away, walked away from me and stood at the window, looking outside. He fidgeted with his hands and refused to look at me.

"Kevin... I know you don't talk about this a lot—"

"About what?"

"About your first girlfriend, Mariah—"

"Don't you fucking say her name, that girl broke my heart, she has nothing to do with this."

"I thought it'd go like this. Kevin, she didn't break your heart. She didn't 'leave you' when you were young. This is all the DCL-36 at work."

"What are you trying to say?"

"You killed Mariah, Kevin. When you were both young. You murdered her for a higher purpose."

My world is spinning. I am on the floor. I am driving off of the Old Iron Bridge. I am drowning in my car. I am kissing Sara. I am fucking Mariah. I am working in the shop with Walt. I am watching Jerry bounce on the exercise ball at my old job. I am laughing with Ted at Jerry's antics in a convenience store. I am retrieving mail from a PO box with an old woman watching me, drooling. I am watching through the woods as a young boy, pointing out squirrels and bugs to Mariah. I am sitting in the backseat of a car in high school, as Sara smokes a cigarette in the passenger seat and some punk kid drives us around. I am talking to my mother on the phone as my grandmother makes dinner. But now this memory is tainted by Mitch's words. Is she an actress? Then I'm signing the will and accepting my dead grandmother's house. Did she do it for me, or for the greater good?

"You killed her, Kevin. And now you're going to kill Sara."

I look up.

"No," I stand. "What? How could you say that, as her, as our friend?"

"It's not my doing. And it's not to my liking. But you're protecting a lot of people. And ensuring happiness for a lot more by following through."

"Why? So I can go and be locked up with that old lunatic Banner on the hill?"

"It's... not exactly like that. He's... hell, Kevin. He's in paradise. Whatever Our Protector is offering him beats anything we could achieve here on earth, here in Deptford."

"'Our Protector' – listen to yourself!"

"Kevin, Sal was trying to get you to break the cycle. But that would have caused all of us to die. It might have even ended humanity as we know it. If Our Protector rises, who knows where his rage will end?"

"The protector... You're talking about the big manatee thing?"

"Yes."

"Fuck you, Mitch."

"It's true, Kevin. Let me guess? Sal gave you a bunch of stories that you ignored. Stories about lovers and failed kings and princes? And he told you to distance yourself from Sara or love her too, right? He was trying to break the cycle. If you loved her, you wouldn't kill her, and if you weren't near her, there was no sacrifice. If He rose, Sal would burn with the rest of us."

"But why would he do that?"

"Perhaps serving is not satisfactory enough for some people."

I sat down.

"Listen, Kevin," he said. "You can meet us at the fairgrounds tonight and see to your duties. Or I'll see you in hell."

Mitch went to the kitchen and washed his hands, forearms, neck, and face. As he opened the front door, he paused and looked at me.

"I know it's not easy. But it's how we fit into this world. We are pieces in a greater machine. And you are more than welcome to defect. Just remember at what cost. Oh, and that pink stuff that that tweaker gave you? It's legit. If you want to clear your mind a bit..." he shrugged and left, pulling his hood up as he closed the door.

CHAPTER THIRTY

I removed the top of the vial, poured a line of the powder onto my wrist, and snort it, quickly, entirely, wholly.

For a moment, I am blinded. Then the room is over-exposed and bleeding white, bleeding light. Then all the lines form again and every hard surface is highlighted in a black, bold line. Colors become more significant and I take a seat. The bruise on the back of my head and the areas that were in pain during my previously-experienced drug-induced migraines begin twitching. At first, it's a bit painful, but then it becomes rehabilitating. I close my eyes and I feel as if the compartments of my brain are expanding, as if the damage and pain done is being pushed outward, is healing, is disappearing.

Every hour of my life lost due to the blue substance is being rebuilt by the pink. I remember, weeks ago, hosting a meeting of the conservation society. I remember talking to Sara about Mariah. I remember shaking Ted's hand at one of the meetings. Ted. Ted was one of them. So was I. I remember visiting my grandfather, Old Joe Banner, at the castle. He's in a chair, sitting, smiling, comatose, looking out the window. I remember visiting my grandmother's grave, Walt's grave, with Sal and Margaret. I was very, very busy in the second month of my coma. You know, the one that no one else remembers, but me. There's a reason so many people insisted I was in a coma for a month.

What else did I do that this drug couldn't retrieve? Who did I help? Who did I hurt? Every dream I've had during the past year rapidly shoots back behind my eyes. I think of the college girl I hooked up with from the bar. I think of her roommate who was incredibly judgmental of me and my age and who had a killer body. Why did it have to be Sara who was a part of the cycle and not some anonymous lay like that drunk girl? Did I have it in me to kill someone, especially a woman I had feelings for? Fuck, I've done it already, apparently. I murdered the one person on this earth that I truly loved. I acted as a pawn, because it served some pagan-bullshit god.

All these people were expecting me to kill Sara. It was as simple as getting the mail or taking out the trash. This was a part of our routine. This promised our continued existence. And I was only voluntarily a part of it as of a few hours ago. This was not the free-will that Western society had promised me, growing up. I got to my bedroom to get changed and I find a shoebox on my dresser. There is a note that reads: In case it makes it easier. –Joe and an insufferable smiley face. I open the shoebox and a loaded revolver awaits me.

Sara calls me a few hours later and asks if I want to go to the County Fair tonight. I say yes. She tells me she will get me.

I am wearing a sweater vest, a button down shirt and tie, and I have the gall to cover it all in a generic grey hoodie. It may be raining, after all. The revolver is concealed, tucked inside my waistband.

Sara gets me and we both know what is happening. We are going to the County Fair, but as the festivities progress and the children eat cotton candy and the men and women get drunk off of the beer stands, handfuls of us will be in the woods worshipping a flying paper mache creature. And I am supposed to kill Sara. Does she know this? Is she willing? Will I destroy the universe if I mention this to her; would some sort of paradox be manifested if I broke the news, especially if she was ignorant of it?

I hold out.

We park on the grass and my heart is in my throat. The weight of the gun presses against me and we get out of the car. She is gorgeous in the moonlight, her eyes seemingly larger and lined in black makeup and she is, good Christ, wearing one of my thermal shirts, a purple one she got me for Christmas a few years ago. The sensation that we've all been here before strikes me for a moment and I wish I had more of the pink drug to consume. Delicious, liberating, DCL-34.

We follow the throngs of eager civilians towards the sparkling lights of the fairgrounds and break off just before the entrance, making our way to the woods. No one else seems aware of it, but every so often I detect a primal, deep vibration from under our feet. Something stirs and no one seems to care.

We are eventually alone, following a trail, deep into the woods. She seems to know where we are going more than I do, but my dreams and distant memories seem to be keeping pace, just fine.

"So," she smiles in the darkness and squeezes my hand. "How exactly does this work?"

"Uh," I look at her fair skin, brought out by the full moon over our heads. "You seemed to be the expert. I was given a crash course over the last couple of hours. Do you know, Jerry's dead? So is Sal."

She frowned and looked at our feet as we walked.

Something cracks behind us.

"It's terrible," she said. "But it's what needed to be done."

She coughs and we keep moving.

"How long did you know, Sara?"

We stop and she looks at me.

"Since we were in high school, Kevin."

"And you wanted to be involved?"

"I mean... look at it from my position. We were always close. And once Mariah was out of the picture... the position of 'princess' was open. No more sacrifices. No more blood oaths. Just happily ever after. Look at your grandma. She never had to work, had a wonderful house, and unlimited money—"

"My grandmother died alone and at the end of a weapon, Sara."

"What...?"

"Yeah, I know," I stammered. "Rude fucking awakening, huh?"

At this point, Mitch steps out from the path and nods at us. He tells us that the others will be along shortly. The tremors we both acknowledge let us know that the Protector, "Lenny," is growing restless. I cannot believe that this is my life. We can never properly gauge where will we stand. Very few could even guess this, even at the most extreme extent of binging and philosophizing.

We stand there in silence for a few moments. I choose to sit against the tree and the bright moonlight makes it almost as clear as day. I play with the revolver in my pants and remove it, twirling the dial. I look down the built-on sight and stare at the tree directly across from me.

"Hey, Mitch," I ask.

"Yeah?"

"What would happen if I— I put the gun to my head. If I just ended it."

Mitch moves towards me as the metal touches my skin, but he stops. He begins to pace.

"Well... we'd all die. The Protector would rise. He would scorch the Fairgrounds and then the town. And maybe move onto the rest of humanity after that. The bloodline would be broken and Banner would have been the only one saved."

"So, that's how it works? You buy into this organization, do your dues, and then die? And you transcend to this higher plane of existence?"

"Yes," Mitch agrees. "More or less."

"So if I just offed myself... I might be saved, considering I am a direct heir to Old Joe."

"I... I don't know, Kevin. Don't do anything rash."

"Oh, please, Mitch," I stand and look at Sara. "Sara... why would you want to get mixed into all of this?
She blinks.

"My life was always here, Kev," she whispered. "Plus, I've always had feelings for you."

"Correction," I interjected. "You had feelings for me once Mariah was dead and in the ground."

"No, I..."

"You saw an opportunity. Tell me, why didn't you go and live with that tweaker, Frink, in Seattle, huh? He seemed up your alley? He got away from it. He just gets high with his fucking grandfather all day. Tell me, why didn't you escape?"

"Kevin, please—"

"Shut up. You saw an opportunity. You saw luxury. You were never going to amount to anything so you cornered power in the highest aspect you could ever hope to possibly attain." I again raised the gun to my head. "Tell me, Sara. Were I to blow my brains out, right here and now, what would become of you? You and him," I point to Mitch, "would just become another pair of charred bodies. You wouldn't be anything. You were never anything. Even at the most troubling times in our relationship, never did I think you were truly using me. I supported you the whole time, end-times or not. We always found common ground. But even when we're beyond the whole normal, mortal realm of it all, you were still a conniving, strategizing whore of a person. God damn it. God fucking damn it."
I fire the gun into the tree.

"Fuck, that feels good, Sara. Have you ever fired a gun?" I cross to her and clutch her to my body. I force her hand into mine and we are both holding the gun. I am behind her, as if I am instructing her at a shooting range. Briefly, the gun is pointed at Mitch, but I turn both of our bodies and aim at a tree.
"You see that, Sara?" I fire once. Twice. She whimpers at each shot.
"Do you see how easy it is to fire, to end a life, to dictate motion, to control physical violence?"
I fire once more into the sky.

The moon is incredibly full right now. It is as bright as day, no metaphor needed. More members of the organization come from the surrounding trees. Art is there. He wears a large Bowie knife on his belt that he unsheathes, not threatening me, but offering assistance. He knows that something must occur, one way or the other. A circle is forming around Mitch, Sara, and I. Sara sees this and begins looking for an out.
There is no such luxury.

"Sara," I clear my throat. "Tell me. When, my darling, dearest Mariah died, what did you think? What was your thought process? You thought you could move in with impunity? You thought because my grandmother owned a fucking rancher you could live the high life? How. Terribly. You. Have. Mistaken."

I fire the remaining two shots into a random Society member. The rest do not care. I am their Prince. Royal blood pumps through my veins. It feels good to take life without a veil, without amnesia, without misdirection for once. It feels good, for once, to take credit for one's own actions.

I discard the revolver. Fireworks begin over the County Fair a half a mile over, above the fairgrounds. Children laugh. Ignorant adults clap. Candy is purchased and fried food is made. I look to Art. He tosses me the long-bladed knife. It gleams in the moonlight and I make eye-contact with Sara. She knows what is next. I know what is next. A nameless member of the Society approaches from behind and holds a black duster jacket open for me to step into. I do just that and adjust myself, reclaiming the knife after I am comfortable.

The dream I had forever ago becomes reality. Sara is the fair-skinned girl running wildly through the woods, evading her pursuer, me, donning my ceremonial knife and garb. She runs and I follow, but we all know how it ends. She is dead and I find the black paint in the pocket of the jacket. Art concealed it for my convenience.

There is no hellfire today. There is no apocalypse, yet. There are only a handful of deaths and no one to tell the story.

EPILOGUE

On top of a hill, there sits an assisted living facility which houses all of Deptford County's decrepit, criminally insane, and those elderly beyond help. Some refer to it, charmingly, as the Castle.

At any given moment, there may be nurses dispensing medicine to any given patient, in hopes of calming their nerves and quelling a violent outbreak. This happens during any given day, at any given hour, on any given floor. However, on the top-most floor, on the top of tower, a floor which gives particular credence to the nickname "castle," sit two patients who share the same blood.

Their names are Joseph Banner and Kevin. Kevin's last name is irrelevant. It was a ploy on behalf of the Conservation Society, in hopes of keeping him in the dark and complacent until the time was right. They succeeded.

The nurse delivering medication to the two relatives pushes a cart. The various trays and compartments on the cart are empty. She wears the special medications on her waist, under her apron. She only has this delivery left for the day.

She removes the special vials for Joseph and Kevin. She knocks twice, waits a few seconds for a non-existent response, and enters. Kevin and Joseph sit in rocking chairs, looking out the window over the forests, mountains, cliffs, and coasts of Deptford County. They are not sentient, not in any functional capacity. They are dead to this world. She puts two pills in each of their mouths, DCL-75, and holds a small cup of water to their mouths. She gently holds their heads back and rubs their throats until they swallow, forever smiling, forever gazing out at the landscape.

She bids goodnight to the gentlemen and closes their door. They are in the only room in the facility which has a hardwood finish, an area-rug, and a fireplace. It is a rustic cabin interior within a healthcare facility, within a prison, really.

Behind their glazed stares lies something else. No one on the outside can see it, but they are both seeing the same, beautiful scene.

They are both in Bannersville, forever celebrating a festival with no name. Joseph and Kevin are both on stage, their beloved significant others at their hips. Joseph and his first love, Kevin and his dearest Mariah. They smile and wave at the crowd before them, forever cheering.

These members of the crowd, they are only there in death, or in fleeting bouts of meditation. Sometimes, Kevin recognizes Ted and Mitch in the crowd. Most of the time, they are undetectable figures in a mass. Sometimes, he even recognizes Sal in the far back. But that is uncommon. He does not understand how, but he does not ask. He notices that he never sees Sara, or his grandmother. But this, too, he never bothers to ask about.

Here, they live happily. He loves his grandfather, he loves his adopted grandmother of sorts, and he loves his dearest Mariah. Her kisses are the sweetest he has ever tasted and they are severely lacking the formaldehyde and decay he experienced in nightmares. This is all granted to them by the one that they called "Lenny" back in the realm of the weak-minded.

At night, they retire to their castle of art and beauty. They sleep in their individual chambers, married to their beloveds, and stare out at the dark landscape, purple ash and charcoal gathering in the corners of this hidden realm. Their wives rest comfortably in their ornate beds, waiting for their husbands to retire to sleep. The two men live in separate master bedrooms, but are each identical to one another. Every night, before taking to slumber, they relax before their gigantic fireplaces, bathing in the orange, blue, and purple glow of this universe. They stare at the dark mountain ranges and smile, content. Behind their glazed stares lies something else. No one on the outside can see it, but they are both seeing the same, beautiful scene.

CPSIA information can be obtained
at www.ICGtesting.com
Printed in the USA
BVHW03s1142260418
514515BV00011B/82/P